"I know when a man has kissed me,"

she said to Duke Prescott. But Princess
Meredith Elizabeth Penwyck *wasn't* sure. Not
at all. For all she knew, she might have imagined
that returned pressure of his lips. That sense that
he was kissing her back, feeling some semblance
of the madness that had stricken her. Imagination?
Wishful thinking?

His head lowered an inom
him. "When I d   , I
assure you that

She locked her k   g.
"When?"

"If."

"It's not like you to retreat, Colonel. Or misspeak."

"Of course." His expression was once again
frustratingly inscrutable. "Good morning, then,
Your Royal Highness."

Meredith watched him leave.

When he kissed her?

If only.

Dear Reader,

This May, we celebrate Mother's Day and a fabulous month of uplifting romances. I'm delighted to introduce RITA® Award finalist Carol Stephenson, who debuts with her heartwarming reunion romance, *Nora's Pride*. Carol writes, "*Nora's Pride* is very meaningful to me, as my mother, my staunchest fan and supporter, passed away in May 2000. I'm sure she's smiling down at me from heaven. She passionately believed this would be my first sale." A must-read for your list!

The Princess and the Duke, by Allison Leigh, is the second book in the CROWN AND GLORY series. Here, a princess and a duke share a kiss, but can their love withstand the truth about a royal assassination? We have another heart-thumper from the incomparable Marie Ferrarella with *Lily and the Lawman*, a darling city-girl-meets-small-town-boy romance.

In *A Baby for Emily*, Ginna Gray delivers an emotionally charged love story in which a brooding hero lays claim to a penniless widow who, unbeknownst to her, is carrying *their* child.... Sharon De Vita pulls on the heartstrings with *A Family To Come Home To*, in which a rugged rancher searches for his family and finds true love! You also won't want to miss Patricia McLinn's *The Runaway Bride*, a humorous tale of a sexy cowboy who rescues a distressed bride.

I hope you enjoy these exciting books from Silhouette Special Edition—the place for love, life and family. Come back for more winning reading next month!

Sincerely,

Karen Taylor Richman
Senior Editor

Please address questions and book requests to:
Silhouette Reader Service
U.S.: 3010 Walden Ave., P.O. Box 1325, Buffalo, NY 14269
Canadian: P.O. Box 609, Fort Erie, Ont. L2A 5X3

The Princess and the Duke

ALLISON LEIGH

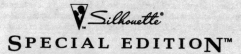

SPECIAL EDITION™

Published by Silhouette Books

America's Publisher of Contemporary Romance

Special thanks and acknowledgment are given
to Allison Leigh for her contribution to the
CROWN AND GLORY series.

 SILHOUETTE BOOKS

ISBN 0-373-24465-7

THE PRINCESS AND THE DUKE

Visit Silhouette at www.eHarlequin.com

Printed in U.S.A.

ALLISON LEIGH

started her career early by writing a Halloween play that her grade-school class performed for her school. Since then, though her tastes have changed, her love for reading has not. And her writing appetite simply grows more voracious by the day.

She has been a finalist for the RITA® Award and the Holt Medallion. But the true highlights of her day as a writer are when she receives word from a reader that they laughed, cried or lost a night of sleep while reading one of her books.

Born in Southern California, she has lived in several different cities in four different states. She has been, at one time or another, a cosmetologist, a computer programmer and a secretary. She has recently begun writing full-time after spending nearly a decade as an administrative assistant for a busy neighborhood church, and currently makes her home in Arizona with her family. She loves to hear from her readers, who can write to her at P.O. Box 40772, Mesa, AZ 85274-0772.

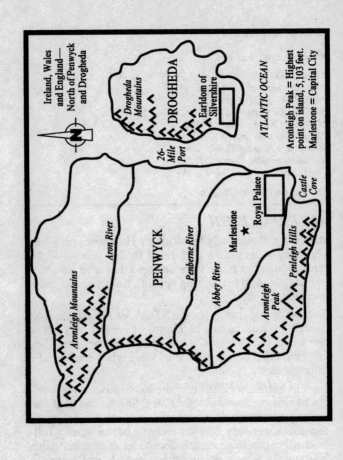

Ireland, Wales and England—North of Penwyck and Drogheda

N

DROGHEDA

Drogheda Mountains

Earldom of Silvershire

ATLANTIC OCEAN

Aronleigh Peak = Highest point on island, 5,103 feet.
Marlestone = Capital City

26-Mile Port

Aron River

PENWYCK

Penberne River

Abbey River

Aronleigh Mountains

Marlestone

Royal Palace

Castle Cove

Aronleigh Peak

Penleigh Hills

Prologue

"I *am* going to dance with him." Meredith's voice was soft, but filled with certainty. She smoothed her hands down the sides of her ball gown. It was the first time she'd been allowed to wear a strapless gown, and the pale, shimmering green fabric clung to her seventeen-year-old curves.

Her sister Anastasia made a skeptical noise beside her. "Then go ask him," she goaded with the tormenting disgust of a sister three years younger. "If you are so certain."

"Be quiet, Ana," hushed Megan, often the voice of reason between her focused, intelligent older sister and her passionately opinionated younger sister. "Meredith, you have every male in this place under thirty years of age practically desperate to dance with you. I'm sure that Lieutenant Prescott feels the same."

"He's old enough to be her father. *And* he is on duty," Anastasia reminded them sarcastically. "Remember?"

"The guards are allowed breaks," Megan countered soothingly.

"Frankly, I can't imagine what the appeal is," Anastasia muttered.

"Keep your voice down, Ana," Meredith warned softly. "Or perhaps you'd like your comments to be printed in tomorrow's papers." *And the Lieutenant is seven years older than I am,* she added silently with a mental, *So there.*

"Exactly," Megan murmured. "The three sisters of Penwyck. Meredith the horny, Megan the boring and Ana the loudmouth."

All three of them giggled, which they quickly curtailed when their mother sent them a long, telling look. They *were* supposed to be listening with dignified grace to their father while he gave his annual welcome to the Royal Spring Ball, not whispering and giggling. Even the boys, Owen and Dylan, despite being only twelve, were behaving more appropriately than the girls.

Meredith leaned over to Megan, who was a few inches shorter. "You're not boring, idiot, and you know it."

"But you *do* want to dance with Lieutenant Prescott," Megan replied, her pretty green eyes laughing. "Is *he* the one who is going to give you your first kiss?"

Meredith felt her cheeks flush and looked guiltily toward the uniformed officer standing at attention near the open terrace doors.

He wore his formal army uniform, all gleaming black and gold buttons. The black beret with the gold trim set upon his head at a serious angle only added to his appeal, as far as Meredith was concerned. His chestnut-colored hair was cut militarily short, yet her fingertips still tingled from fantasizing about the feel of it. She easily imagined the steady weight of his gaze, even though she didn't have a clue where exactly he was looking. The distance from where she stood with her family on the dais at the head of the grand ballroom to where he stood at attention near one of the sets of doors opening onto the starlit terrace was too great.

Silvery-green, she thought with a little sigh. Whether she could see them up close now or not, she knew exactly the shade of his silvery-green eyes. Almost exactly the shade of her gown. "He already did kiss me," she murmured, and then laughed soundlessly at Megan's gasp. "When I was ten, remember? The school did a summer project to rehabilitate that old mill up in the Aronleigh Mountains. His mother coordinated it through her school. I slammed my thumb with a hammer, and he kissed it better." Of course, he'd done that with a great amount of sarcasm because she'd been very much on her royal high horse, but at this moment, she chose to ignore that.

"That's right," Megan whispered, leaning centimeters toward Meredith. "I'd forgotten that his mother was a teacher."

"Both his parents died last year," Meredith murmured, her gaze on the officer. Her heart had ached for his loss. She'd written a personal note to him when she'd learned of the auto accident that had claimed their lives, but hadn't had the nerve to send it. The mere thought of the handsome young man reading words she'd penned had sent her heart into an absolute tailspin.

"Just admit it, Meredith," Anastasia said, needling, "you want to *kiss* him."

Meredith, smiling at the guests who had begun clapping at the conclusion of her father's welcome, reached behind Megan and firmly pinched the back of Ana's arm. Her youngest sister jumped, barely containing a yowl, and glared at Meredith, her vivid blue eyes flashing.

But all three girls went utterly silent when their mother, always strikingly beautiful but tonight looking even more so, glided silently to stand beside them. The massive chandeliers overhead caught the tiara carefully situated in Marissa's upswept hair. A million little lights danced from the jewels among her dark tresses, and for a moment, Meredith found herself watching Lieutenant Prescott through a glittering rainbow.

Her breath caught in her throat, and her heart seemed to stop beating altogether for a long, interminable moment.

He *was* looking at her. She felt it right down to her toes.

Her heart came to life, racing, beating so hard that she felt sure it must be visible from the outside.

She had no intention of admitting it to Anastasia with her silly comments, or to Megan either, for that matter.

But she *did* intend to dance with Lieutenant Pierceson Prescott. And before the evening was out, she was going to get him to kiss her, too.

She would, or she wasn't Her Royal Highness, Meredith Elizabeth, Princess of Penwyck.

Chapter One

Grand bells chimed from every steeple, ringing out a chorus the likes of which the country of Penwyck had not heard in decades. Citizens of the island country lined the streets of the capital city, Marlestone, shouting and clapping and singing and pushing eagerly against the barriers as the anticipated hour drew near.

Some had turned out at the crack of dawn to jostle for a position against those who'd slept on the streets all night long. Though *slept* was undoubtedly overstating it, Meredith thought as she rode along the street, her face stretched into a calm smile. Judging by the elaborate setup some in the crowd possessed, she was certain that more revelry had been going on during the night before her sister's wedding than any sleeping.

Anastasia nudged her foot, her eyes laughing as they passed the last corner before turning up the road that would lead to Marlestone Cathedral. A particularly patriotic fellow with his face painted in red and gold waved madly at their open motorcar as they passed.

The closer they drew to the cathedral, the more closely spaced were the security guards, the less boisterous the crowd became, though spirits were most definitely high. Meredith wiggled her toes in her high-heeled pumps. It didn't matter how well designed the satin shoes were, they still pinched her toes.

But at least she and Anastasia were carried in comfort. The men in the wedding party, including her brother Owen, had already walked under the late-afternoon August sunshine a good half mile on foot to the cathedral. They walked through spotless streets lined with people who were as interested in getting a close-up view of the young man most presumed would one day be king as they were in seeing the bridegroom, Jean-Paul Augustuve, Earl of Silvershire, who hailed from neighboring Drogheda.

Their car drew to a slow, measured stop at the base of the steps leading to the cathedral, and Anastasia stood first, the fabric of her long blue gown unfolding smoothly as she was helped from the vehicle to the pristine stone step. With wisps of hair drifting about her slender neck in the gentle breeze, she was a vision, and the crowds let her know it. They cheered when Anastasia ascended a few steps, then stopped to wait for Meredith.

And why wouldn't they cheer for Anastasia? She was wildly popular. And today she looked very much the princess she was with delicate diamond pins glistening among the curls pinned up in an artfully tousled style.

Aware that she was moving just a little too slowly, Meredith gathered her skirts and stepped from the car. The timing of the processional was all carefully orchestrated, right down to the last minute. Just that morning, she had listened with the rest of the family as they'd been run through the drill as if it were a military maneuvering of the highest order.

Despite the fact that Penwyck was on the cusp of signing groundbreaking alliances with a neighboring island country, Majorco, and an even more important alliance with the United States, every branch of the Penwyckian military had given support to the first royal wedding Penwyck had seen since that of the King. There had been a run-through the previous day, without any family members present, of course, to ensure that the timing of everything—from the speed of the motorcars during the procession to the trumpet fanfare when the King arrived with Megan to the gait of the horses that would pull the carriages used during the recession—was spot on.

Meredith sighed a little as she joined Anastasia on the steps to the ornate west entrance to the cathedral. It was hard not to be moved by the bells ringing out so joyfully. And she was very happy for Megan. Of course she was. Megan was in love, and Jean-Paul returned it. What more could a woman ask? Even a princess, blessed with untold privilege, deserved love.

Yet there was a little part deep inside Meredith that was, well, a bit envious. She'd never had a man look at her with his heart in his eyes the way Jean-Paul

looked at Megan. She'd never been swept away by
passion the way Megan and Jean-Paul had been, ev-
idenced by the fact that the heirloom wedding gown
Megan was wearing had had to be carefully altered
to hide her slightly thickening midriff.

At the thought of a coming niece or nephew, Meredith forgot her envy, as she always did. Megan
would be a wonderful mother.

"I'll be lucky if I don't fall flat on my face with
these shoes. I shouldn't have let you talk me into
wearing such high heels," Anastasia murmured under
her breath as they left the brilliant sunshine and entered the wide entrance of the cathedral.

"You can't wear riding clothes *all* the time," Meredith countered easily through her smile. "And keep
your voice down. There are television cameras watching all this, remember?" She didn't know the name
of the young army officer who extended his arm to
escort her along the nave past rows and rows of
guests, then beneath the soaring arch into the more
intimate choir, and even farther up three shallow marble steps to the seats where, for generations, the royal
family had sat near the chancel.

It was a long walk. And for a moment, Meredith
wondered how Megan would fare, as her sister was
still touched by a bit of morning sickness now and
again. Not to mention her recent, frightening brush
with encephalitis.

But Megan would be supported by their father. And
King Morgan was more than able to escort petite
Meggie.

Her escort's job finished, Meredith automatically

held her heavy silk skirt with one hand and turned toward her seat.

But the unexpected sight of the man sitting in the row beside that seat brought her up short. Her feet, inside her slightly pinching priceless pumps took root right there on the polished floor. *"You."*

The uniformed man rose, politely offering his hand to help her up the step to her seat. Feeling foolish, as Anastasia had gracefully stepped around her and was already slipping into the wooden bench that gleamed from years of loving attention, Meredith swallowed and rested her fingers lightly on his hard, warm hand, quickly moving up the step.

Just as quickly, she removed her hand from his as she seated herself. "Thank you, Colonel Prescott," she said politely. "I didn't expect to see you here today."

"Your Royal Highness." He inclined his head as he greeted her. Barely an inch. Just enough to show his respect of her status. Just enough to let her know he was a man who really bowed to no one except perhaps the King.

And why would he? He was the Duke of Aronleigh, after all. An award of great merit bestowed on him by her father a decade earlier.

"I didn't expect to be seated up here, either." His big hand casually brushed aside a fold of her pale gold skirt as he sat beside her. "You're looking as lovely as ever."

Meredith's smile felt strained. "Thank you. Your troops are looking very smart today." He made a soft sound. Almost of impatience, she thought. "You didn't bring a date?"

At that, she did feel his silvery-green gaze turn her way. "I'm hardly here in a social capacity."

Her eyebrow rose. "Are you armed to the teeth then, Colonel, beneath that dress uniform of yours? Prepared to do battle against any interlopers set on disrupting the nuptials?"

His bland expression changed not a whit. Perhaps that *was* what made him such an exceptional colonel. He *was* head of Royal and Army Intelligence, after all, and a member of the Royal Elite Team—a small group of men personally selected by the King as his closest advisers. He was no longer a mere lieutenant standing post at a spring ball. He was a powerful man in his own right.

A man who made her nerves feel as if they were being tormented by a horde of buzzing bees.

"If you are unhappy with the seating arrangement, I'd be happy to sit elsewhere," he assured her evenly.

Meredith stifled the impulse to kick his shin. He *knew* she was uncomfortable sitting beside him. Since her seventeenth year, in fact, she'd gone out of her way to avoid him. And he her. Unfortunately, over the years there'd been many occasions not in the least bit social when they'd had to deal with one another.

"Not at all," she assured him blithely. "Goodness knows how many meetings it took for the seating arrangement to be finalized." She opened her ivory program and stared blindly at the golden script. Jean-Paul's parents had just been seated across the wide aisle, and Meredith smiled and nodded their way. Prince Bernier, the ruler of Drogheda, was seated near them. He was Jean-Paul's uncle, and rumor had it that Jean-Paul might become his uncle's heir, as Bernier only had one daughter. A flighty nut who Meredith had little use for. As far as she was concerned, Bernier could do no better than Jean-Paul. He'd make a fine ruler one day.

Any minute, she knew her mother would be seated, and judging by the sudden hush that fairly echoed up to the lofty mural-painted ceilings of the cathedral, Queen Marissa was undoubtedly even now gliding down the center aisle to the accompaniment of the understated prelude.

As many times as Meredith had practiced that walk as a youth, she'd never figured out how her mother was able to accomplish it. As if she were floating, hovering an inch above the ground as she moved.

Considering the people of her country thought Queen Marissa no less than a living angel, it was an apt thought.

Only it was also a thought that led Meredith to wonder what exactly the man beside her thought. She wasn't thrilled to be seated beside him. Was stunned, in fact, to see him at all. Because, unless it was strictly required of him in his official capacity to attend an event where any member of the royal family was to be present, he avoided it like the plague.

She closed her program and folded her hands on top of it in her lap. If the wedding hadn't been planned in such a rush—an unheard of three weeks, actually—she supposed she might have taken the time to review the seating arrangements and been better prepared. "If not social," she said, determined to remain pleasant, "then it must be official?"

She'd never know if he intended to answer, for her

mother came into view, and everyone rose in deference to her.

Meredith sighed again. Beauty radiated from her mother in a way Meredith could never hope to emulate. It came from inside her, she was sure. And Marissa probably never had feelings of envy for a sister on the happiest day of her life.

Only Marissa had never *had* any sisters. She'd only had one brother, Edwin, and he'd been killed on neighboring Majorco ten years earlier.

"It's a shame my uncle isn't alive to be here today," Meredith murmured as the Queen was seated in one of the two seats closest to the high altar. A uniform shuffle could be heard as everyone followed suit.

"Why?"

She looked at the colonel. Then just as quickly looked away. It was too hard to look at him without getting that infuriatingly breathless feeling inside her chest. "How can you ask that?"

"You were barely eighteen when your uncle died. How well did you even know him?"

Her lips parted. She was as much startled by his awareness of just how old she'd been as she was by his cool tone, which seemed almost a dismissal of the tragedy. "I...well, I remember him from my childhood, of course." Her uncle Edwin had bounced her on his knee and told her tales of knights and dragon slayers. When she was a teenager, he'd been a less frequent visitor. "I was referring to my mother, in any case. He was the last of her side of the family. This is the first wedding of one of her children. I'd think you'd be more sensitive to that since you lost your only family, too.''

''My parents died long ago.''

''Twelve years.'' He wasn't the only one who had a long memory.

His gaze sharpened. ''I'm surprised you remember that.''

''I remember many things,'' Meredith said smoothly. She also remembered the spring following his loss. When he'd succeeded in making her feel a humiliated fool on the dance floor of the Royal Spring Ball.

''How is your sister feeling?''

If he could be polite, so, certainly, could she. She could hide her agitation. Of course she could. ''Megan is doing well. Quite recovered. Thank you for asking.'' Her fingertips toyed with the parchment edge of the program. Only in his company had she ever had to scramble for topics of conversation. ''Plans for the children's facility at the base are going well.''

''So I've heard.''

Meredith's position as the royal family's liaison to the Royal Intelligence Institute kept her closely involved in several efforts of the world-renowned institution. One of the latest was Horizons, a child-care and activity center located on the army base in the north-central portion of Penwyck. ''Will you be at the opening celebration next week?''

''No.''

She didn't know whether it was relief or disappointment that she felt. But a rustling from the vestry heralded the entrance of Jean-Paul and his supporters as they took their place in the chancel, and she focused her attention on the men.

Behind her, Anastasia leaned forward and murmured in her ear that Owen looked particularly smashing in his formal wear.

Meredith had to agree. Her little brother would probably be king one day—though her father had yet to officially name which of his twin sons would be his successor even though Owen was a more natural leader than Dylan. Looking at Owen, she thought the mantle of authority already sat well on his broad shoulders, despite his mere twenty-three years.

"It's a shame Dylan isn't here," Anastasia whispered. "I still can't believe no one has been able to get hold of him."

Meredith nodded. Owen's twin was roaming the hills of Europe somewhere and had completely missed the recent scandal of quiet Megan's stunning revelation of being pregnant.

A sudden muted roar made itself heard from outside the cathedral, and to a one, every guest inside the soaring structure felt a surge of excitement in that half moment before the Royal Trumpet Corp burst into the first brilliant notes of the fanfare that had been written specifically in honor of Megan's wedding. Meredith knew what that cheer meant, what that fanfare meant. It meant that Megan, on the arm of their father, King Morgan of Penwyck, had ascended the steps and was waiting in the cathedral entry.

Shivers danced down her spine. She couldn't help it. Her little sister was getting *married*.

The moment the fanfare concluded, the processional began. The congregation rose again as the low tones from the pipe organ, overlaid with the beautiful, stately notes of a lone trumpeter, soared through the cathedral.

Within minutes, Megan and the King came into view. Meredith's eyes stung as she blinked back tears. Meggie looked beautiful. Simply beautiful. And their father had an uncharacteristically broad smile on his handsome face.

Behind Megan and the King trailed the three little girls who were serving as bridesmaids and the matching three young page boys. They looked sweet as could be, and for a moment, Meredith remembered when she'd been a young girl, participating in some distant relative's wedding.

She glanced over her shoulder at Anastasia, smiling shakily at seeing her feelings mirrored on her sister's face. Anastasia caught Meredith's hand in hers and squeezed. Her striking blue gaze flickered to the groom, and Meredith followed the gaze. A look of adoration and, well, *hunger* shone from Jean-Paul's handsome face.

"He loves her."

Meredith swallowed, surprised at the soft comment coming from the colonel. "Of course he does. Why would we be here today if he didn't?"

Pierce thought about answering that, but decided it would be wiser if he didn't. There was nothing he wouldn't do for the sake of the royal family, nothing he hadn't done for them already. But everyone in the country had been witness to the scandal surrounding Megan and Jean-Paul's engagement. Thanks to the oft invasive media, what should have been a private matter between Her Royal Highness and her lover had instead been splashed across newspapers from one shore of the isle to the other. Pierce knew there had been pressure on the couple to make things right. And though he'd rather chew nails than admit it, he was pleased for the quiet middle princess that this marriage was based in love and not a result of public or private pressure.

But while Princess Megan did make a lovely bride, Pierce was more interested in studying the man escorting her down the aisle.

His Majesty looked much as he always did. Instead of his typical attire, in honor of the occasion he wore his full regalia, complete with the orders of his ancestors pinned to his royal white sash and his lapels emblazoned with the dozens of military medals he'd earned over his career before his coronation. Not a strand of his short, wavy brown hair looked out of place, something the tall, commanding figure carried off without looking the least bit plastic.

Pierce watched the King closely as they neared the chancel. He had just the right amount of emotion in his eyes as he drew the filmy veil from Megan's face, kissed her lightly on the cheek and took his place next to the Queen.

A soft sniffle near his shoulder dragged at his attention, and he looked at Meredith. He knew she topped the five feet mark by exactly seven inches in her bare feet—there were very few details regarding any member of the royal family he wasn't privy to—but in her high heels, she was only a few inches below his six one.

She was tall enough to fit him. Endowed with enough curves to be dangerous to a man's peace of mind. She had a wicked intelligence, eyes the color of emeralds and a mouth made for sin.

Meredith Elizabeth, Princess of Penwyck. Eldest child of the monarch. He'd felt the sting of want for her when she'd been a mere teenager and he a young army officer. Back then, when life was easier, it was her royal status and youth that had kept her out of his reach.

Now, more than a dozen years and an eternity of actions later, she was even more out of his reach. Every time she looked at him with her green eyes, he felt damned. Damned for wanting her. Damned for lying to her. Damned because every time they were within ten yards of one another, he could see the confusion and hurt deep in her eyes that told him she was every bit as aware of him as he was aware of her. And that his deliberate evasion of her hurt.

He glanced at the King and wished to heaven that he could have come up with some reason to avoid this wedding, the way he avoided most all of the social events involving the royal family. The sooner he got away from them all, the better.

But it really wasn't them all that caused his current consternation. It was only the woman beside him who was upsetting his equilibrium.

His mind not at all on the service, Pierce silently offered his handkerchief. She looked at him, surprised, then hurriedly looked away. He watched her suck in her lower lip for a moment, blinking rapidly as she tried to gain control of her emotions. But it was no good. A diamond-bright tear slipped down her ivory cheek.

Almost defiantly, then, she took the square of cloth,

being careful not to touch him in any way as she did so. She quickly dabbed the corners of her eyes, then held out his handkerchief.

The last time he'd seen Meredith so open with her emotions, she'd been seventeen. Back then, it had been all he could do to remember just who she was and keep his behavior properly circumspect. With age, it was easier to remember who she was but no less difficult to remain unmoved by her presence. "Keep it."

She didn't look at him. But her fingers closed over the square of white cloth, enfolding it in her fist.

The organ suddenly blasted the first notes of a hymn. Beside him, Meredith started, betraying her preoccupation.

She was watching the ceremony, crying tears over it, yet she'd been as unprepared for the hymn as he'd been. Because of it, he knew she'd been as lost in her thoughts—whatever they might be—as he'd been in his.

He also realized that the ceremony was nearly finished. For the couple had already retreated and returned from the vestry, along with the bishop and the King and Queen, where they had signed the register. He, master of intelligence, keeper of lies, committer of sins, had managed to miss the entire thing. All because of a woman whose waist he could span with his hands.

The congregation was singing the final hymn. The words came automatically to Pierce, without thought. And thank God—no pun intended—for it.

Considering he'd spent his entire childhood from eight to eighteen with his hind planted in one of the pews of his father's church every Sunday morning and every Wednesday evening, he ought to know the hymns. He ought to know every in and out of every religious service in which the church could possibly participate.

It really was a measure of the powerful distraction standing beside him that he didn't even *think* about what all was involved with a Penwyckian wedding.

Or what sitting beside *her* meant in relation to those details.

Not until the bishop had pronounced Megan and Jean-Paul husband and wife did it begin to dawn on him. Not until Jean-Paul had kissed his new bride, restrained and befitting the public setting but nonetheless a testament to the feelings that ran deep inside him for the woman carrying his child, did it fully hit Pierce.

But by then, it was already too late.

For the bishop, all smiles despite the pomp and circumstance of the event, looked at the congregation. "And now," he intoned, "as has been our custom for centuries, we invite you to greet your neighbors in this house of God with all good grace, and peace, that we may go out into the world, sharing the blessings of this day with all those we meet."

In some countries, Pierce knew sharing the blessing might involve little more than a handshake and a muttered, "Blessin's to yer."

In Penwyck, however, it meant the worst of all possible things as far as Pierce was concerned.

It meant a kiss.

Chapter Two

He'd been the son of a clergyman. Had even, briefly, considered following in his father's stead. How could he have forgotten? How could he have overlooked this one small, fateful detail?

Why hadn't it occurred to him what sitting next to Meredith at the wedding ceremony would entail?

Nerves strung tighter than piano wire, Pierce turned to the elderly woman on his left. She was a countess from somewhere in Belgium, but he'd be blasted if he could remember just where. Until Meredith and Anastasia had entered the church, she'd been busy reminiscing in her slightly shrill voice about the wedding of the King and Queen, thirty-five years earlier.

She'd rattled on and on until Pierce had wanted to put a muzzle on her. Particularly when she'd gone on to the tragedy of "poor, dear Edwin's senseless killing.'' But he could hardly be rude to the woman and tell her he wasn't the least bit interested in hearing about that particular event.

Smiling tightly at the elderly woman, he bussed her on first one heavily powdered cheek, then the other. She smiled beneficently at him and patted his cheek as if he were five instead of thirty-five.

And then Pierce turned to face Meredith. Her tears had dried, and her expression was cool as she stared at him. Then she regally lifted her chin just a hair.

It was rare for Pierceson Prescott to be rattled. But he was now. And that cool movement of Meredith's, that regal little tilt started a slow burn deep down inside him.

All around them, people were greeting each other, laughing and delighting over the lovely quaint custom, but Pierce was aware of none of it. For the world had shrunk to an impossibly small bubble. Containing only him and the woman beside him.

A woman who, he would swear his army commission on, was watching him with challenge lighting her green eyes.

What Pierce wanted to do was sink his fingers into the rich brown waves of her hair, tumbling it from the roll into which it was pinned at her nape, and explore every inch of her mouth with his.

But he wouldn't. He couldn't. She was a member of the royal family, which was his duty and honor to protect and serve. Nor could he ignore the custom, not when it was entirely likely that it would be noticed. There were television cameras posted in the rafters of the cathedral watching every move of the royals and those nearby, for God's sake!

Jaw aching, he lowered his head those few inches and touched Meredith's cheek with his lips, barely grazing the satiny skin. And in return, he felt her lips, feather-light and soft as a dream, against his tight jaw.

Trembling like a leaf, Meredith nearly sighed aloud when Pierce's lips touched her cheek. The brief moment seemed to stretch into an eternity as they parted. Anyone else would have simply kissed the other cheek and been done with it.

But not with Pierce. Never with Pierce.

Her gaze was caught in his, and her stomach tumbled a mile at the dark flame that seemed to burn in his. Her lungs felt starved for air, her heart starved for blood. And then, without conscious thought, she tilted her head and touched his lips with hers. Briefly, so very briefly.

Yet she felt him go stock-still. Felt the harsh inhalation of his breath after that first moment of shock passed. Felt the press of his lips against hers in that fraction of a second, demanding and hot.

Her lips softened, parted. Clung as the kiss threatened to go deeper. Shocked to the core at her own daring, she hastily stepped away, looking everywhere but at him, struggling to catch her breath.

The bride and groom had moved around in the chancel, all smiles. Megan swept into a low, utterly graceful curtsy to her father, the King, and Jean-Paul bowed. Then the triumphant strains of the recessional rang through the church, and they began their walk down the aisle, this time as husband and wife.

The bishop followed, along with the King and Queen. Then Jean-Paul's supporters. Anastasia surreptitiously jostled Meredith's arm, giving her an odd look, and realizing that she was hanging back, Meredith quickly ordered her shaking legs to move and stepped out of the pew to take her place in line as the family left the cathedral.

She didn't look at the colonel.

She didn't dare.

The light breeze had deepened to a cool wind, and when she stepped through the entrance onto the steps outside the cathedral, she had to catch her skirts from being blown around her knees. If the crowd had been boisterous before the ceremony, now they were positively wild as the bridal couple descended the stairs and entered the first horse-drawn coach, which would transport them through the central streets of Marlestone before making its way to the palace where the reception was being held in the grand ballroom.

The King and Queen were in the next coach, this one glass-enclosed, unlike the open-air one the bridal couple occupied. Then came their own carriage, Owen joining them for the return trip. The young bridesmaids and page boys went last, and Meredith, who was facing the rear, watched with a faint smile as little Sarah Julia flounced into her seat and waved at the crowds as if she were the Queen herself. There was a fleet of waiting motorcars to carry Jean-Paul's parents, Prince Bernier and the other visiting royals to the palace.

There would be no good-natured scrambling for rides at this wedding. It was too well orchestrated.

Meredith's gaze drifted up the steps to the guests who were beginning to stream from the cathedral doors, and like a homing pigeon, her attention went straight to Colonel Prescott, who stood on the topmost step, a bit aside from the throng. Her breath caught in her throat.

He was watching her ride away.

Anastasia nudged Owen and laughed softly. "Methinks our fair Meredith has a crush. Still."

Owen raised one eyebrow and glanced over his shoulder. A gaggle of teenagers lining the street nearby screamed as if he were the latest pinup, but he gave no notice. He looked at Meredith. "Who, Prescott? He's a good man."

"I'm twenty-eight years old," Meredith said flatly. "Far too old for crushes."

Anastasia smiled impishly. "What about—" she waited a beat "—*love?*"

Meredith deliberately ignored her sister.

"You should have seen the kiss she planted on the man," Anastasia pseudo whispered to Owen. "Everyone in the cathedral could feel the heat, and it had nothing to do with the sunlight coming through the stained-glass windows *or* the way Jean-Paul devours Megan with his eyes."

Meredith's cheeks burned. "Don't be ridiculous," she said more sharply than she intended.

Anastasia's grin gentled. She could be a holy terror, but she was utterly softhearted. "Meredith, I'm only teasing you. I know how you feel about the colonel. Honestly, where is your sense of humor today?"

"I don't feel *anything* about the colonel," Meredith said flatly. "And I really do wish you'd drop it."

Anastasia did, but Meredith could feel her sister's pensive gaze on her for the remainder of the ride through the city. By the time the carriage passed through the massive gates leading to the palace, Meredith felt well and truly shrewish. She waited until they'd alighted from the carriage and caught Ana's hand, squeezing it. "I'm sorry," she whispered.

Her sister smiled faintly, but there was little time to go into it, for the wedding guests were converging on the palace at an alarming rate. Meredith, who was used to playing the role of hostess at any number of royal functions, gathered her skirts and, putting Pierceson Prescott out of her mind—as far as he would go, at any rate—swept up the palace stairs and through the grand hall, greeting guests while subtly maneuvering them toward the ballroom and away from the doors to alleviate the bottleneck that occasionally formed there.

She was supposed to have gone straight to the private quarters where the official photographer planned to take a few photos, but knowing what a madhouse *that* was likely to be, she decided the staff needed her help in the ballroom more.

She didn't let herself dwell on the fact that, while she was greeting and herding guests, there was no sign of Colonel Prescott.

The orchestra was playing, and the solemnity of the ceremony was fading as the noise level rose in the ballroom. It didn't matter what one's heritage was, royal or common. A party was a party was a party.

And this one was undoubtedly going to be a grand one.

But before the royal family could truly participate, there were those formal photos to be taken, and Meredith was one of the last to skip up to the balcony where the bride and groom had gathered, along with both sets of parents, cousins, distant or otherwise, and a veritable horde of other people.

"There you are, darling," the Queen greeted Meredith when she'd finally extricated herself from the guests and arrived. "I was about to send Gwen after you."

Meredith dashed a smoothing hand over her hair and with barely a blink slid into her customary position, behind and to the left of the Queen and King, who were always in the center of every photo but today would step toward the side in honor of the bridal couple.

She hid a smile at the way Jean-Paul and Megan's hands were wound together, all but hidden by the drape of Megan's dress. Meredith was long used to endless photography sessions, and her mind wandered as the photographer put them through their poses. Then it was out to the balcony over the ballroom where Megan and Jean-Paul smiled and waved and pleased the crowds waiting outside the palace gates by kissing each other.

It was joyful and great fun, and by the time the family descended the elegant stairs from the upper story to the ballroom proper, Meredith felt a little refreshed.

Which was a good thing, because judging by the revelers inside the ballroom, it looked to be a long evening ahead of them.

There was still the sit-down dinner, for one thing. For approximately five hundred of the couple's nearest and dearest. The food was delicious, as was everything that came from the palace kitchens. From starters of smoked salmon canapés and delicate Gruyère and spinach tarts, through herb-stuffed veal to the finish of crème brulée and the official royal wedding cake that had taken two full weeks to prepare in the highly secured culinary institute affiliated with the Royal Intelligence Institute. It was all delicious.

Only Meredith could have been eating sawdust for all the notice she took of it, thanks to the seating arrangements. She'd had more than enough shocks for the day when it came to Colonel Pierceson Prescott. Seeing him in the cathedral at all was the first. Then that ridiculous insanity of hers that led her to actually *kiss* the man was next. But to find out that he had come to the palace for the reception while she'd been busy upstairs with the photography session was even more of a shock.

She couldn't recall the last time Pierceson Prescott had stepped foot in the palace, though she supposed he certainly must have done so at some point since he'd been awarded his dukedom all those years ago. He had frequent dealings with the King, after all.

Meredith let her mind puzzle over his absences for some time, mostly because it was safer to concentrate on that than succumb to the memory of the feel of his lips or the warmth of his breath on her cheek in the cathedral.

Never in her life had she been so preoccupied with another individual. She was also quite sure she didn't like being preoccupied. She could only hope it was because of the rarity of his presence.

Instead of the traditionally long banquet tables, the ballroom was filled with round tables to accommodate the number of guests, with the bride and groom and their parents at the long head table on the dais. The rest of the family were interspersed about the room, and Meredith thought that if it weren't for Megan's happiness, she'd have had to have had a serious word with her middle sister about the planning that had gone into the seating arrangements. For she was seated directly opposite Colonel Pierceson Prescott.

Admittedly, there were six other individuals at the table, as well, two married couples who were distantly related to Jean-Paul, an eligible single man and an equally eligible single woman who was doing a bang-up job of flirting with Colonel Prescott.

She stifled a sigh and dug her fork into the incredibly rich confection of cream cake and delicate fresh raspberries that the culinary institute had created for the wedding cake. No rum cake for Megan—she'd overruled that typical selection because of her pregnancy.

Keeping half an ear out for the toasts that were being made, she surreptitiously slid her heels out of her shoes. It was safe enough in light of the ivory and royal-blue linens that swept to the marble floor.

What she really wanted to do far more than wiggle her toes, however, was toss her linen napkin across the table to cover the low-cut bodice of Juliet Oxford. She was leaning toward the colonel, undoubtedly giving him quite an eyeful.

The man beside Meredith said something, and she murmured an absent assent, only to realize a half second later that she'd unthinkingly agreed to have dinner with him. His narrow face gleamed with a broad smile, and Meredith squelched yet another sigh. She couldn't back out. It would be utterly rude.

Her cheeks heated, however, when she caught the

colonel's amused gaze. As if he knew exactly what had transpired to lead her into an unwanted dinner engagement.

Her smile firmed, and she ignored the colonel. "If you'd be good enough to call my personal secretary tomorrow, George, we'll settle on a date."

George smiled winningly. Meredith *would* go out to dinner with the man, and she *would* have a perfectly lovely time. George Valdosta was a few years older than she was, and she'd known him practically forever. He was well read, had a decent sense of humor and—

—wasn't Pierceson Prescott.

She picked up her champagne and smiled brightly at George, determined to ignore the little voice inside her that insistently compared George's modest appeal with the colonel's overwhelming magnetism. It wasn't George's fault he wasn't as tall as the colonel. Or that his thinning blond hair wasn't the rich chestnut the colonel kept rigidly cut in order to control the lustrous waves. George couldn't help the fact that his blue eyes were just that. Blue. Ordinary and not the least bit full of anything that seemed to speak to her soul.

Annoyed with herself more than ever, the moment the speeches were completed and the orchestra began playing again, Meredith drained her champagne and practically leaped from her chair to drag poor George through the tables to the dance floor.

The bride and groom danced first, of course, but were soon joined by the King and Queen. The guests stood on ceremony only long enough to receive an invitation to the gleaming dance floor from King Morgan before they crowded on. It didn't matter whether it was a stately waltz, a smooshy love song or the latest rock hit from America, Meredith thought, as she swung in George's arms to the quick tempo. These people were ready to dance.

Not even the departure of Megan and Jean-Paul dimmed the celebration, Meredith noticed later, as she hovered in the private courtyard. The limousine that would carry the couple to the private port where Jean-Paul's sailing ketch, the *West Wind,* was docked had long departed. But Meredith had little desire to go back to the reception, though she knew she should.

"Quit mooning." Anastasia slid her arm through Meredith's and leaned close as they finally turned and headed toward the ballroom through the formal gardens. "They're honeymooning at sea. It's very romantic."

"Yes."

"And you're going to miss Meggie."

"Yes."

Anastasia sighed a little. "I will, too." But she brightened almost immediately. "So, any smoldering looks from our lovely Duke of Aronleigh across the dinner table this evening?"

"Anastasia, please."

"What? The man looks at you as if he is mentally salivating."

Meredith's cheeks heated, and she was glad the only light in the gardens came from the plethora of tiny white bulbs twinkling in the trees. But, as she and her sister were utterly alone, she couldn't keep her thoughts in any longer. "If Colonel Prescott had ever been the least bit interested in me, he would have said or done something long before now. He's a man of action, Anastasia.''

"Mmm. Brings delicious things to mind, doesn't it?'' Her sister giggled softly, reminding Meredith of the teenager she'd once been. "Yet he usually doesn't make appearances at our humble abode. And he's here tonight. Sitting right across from you.''

"Coincidence,'' Meredith assured her. "Mark my words. When we go back into the ballroom, I'll bet you my favorite bottle of perfume he'll be dancing with Juliet Oxford.''

"With her surgically enhanced chest, you mean.''

"Anastasia!''

Her sister shrugged, uncaring. "It's true, isn't it? Though Juliet certainly didn't begin there. She started with that nose. And the chin, and then her buggy eyes—''

"You're awful.'' Meredith couldn't help but laugh at her sister's outrageous statements. Juliet Oxford may have had some help in the cleavage department, but she'd been born beautiful, and Anastasia knew it.

Her sister grinned, then pulled Meredith toward the steps leading to the terrace. "Seriously, darling, why would the duke possibly want her when he could have you? He is probably here because of the action you took at the church with that kiss.''

Meredith appreciated her sister's loyalty, but not necessarily the reminder of her behavior. The doors to the ballroom were open to take advantage of the lovely night, and music streamed from inside. They paused in the doorway, taking in the sight of the guests. The Queen had retired to her chambers after bidding goodbye to Megan and Jean-Paul. Jean-Paul's parents had also departed, along with a good number of the older guests. Those who remained seemed fit to party until dawn, including the King, who was standing in conversation with a small group of people near the dais. As Meredith watched, her father tossed back his head and laughed uproariously.

Well, at least he was having a good time. Taking a small breather from the stress of the last several weeks while negotiating the alliances.

Only Meredith wasn't interested in watching her father. After that one brief glance, her eyes had immediately trained on Pierceson Prescott. Who was, sure enough, on the dance floor, holding Juliet Oxford in his arms. "What did I tell you?" Meredith murmured to her sister. The smile on her face felt unusually forced.

Anastasia gave her a sympathetic look before being swept off by friends. Meredith headed for one of the liveried staff circulating the room and took a crystal flute from his tray.

In seconds, George was at her side, but she begged off dancing, holding up her champagne. "I think I'd like just a quiet spot for a bit, George, if you don't mind?"

Far too good-natured to be offended, he offered his company. She could hardly decline, but she was utterly grateful when some of his friends soon came by and pulled him away. Then, while she was rather stealthily working her way toward the terrace and the peace and quiet out there, Owen looped his arm around her waist.

She barely had time to put down her glass before

he swung her onto the dance floor. "You can't rebuff your brother," he said, grinning.

"Well, I *could*," Meredith corrected, grinning back. "But I wouldn't want to embarrass you in front of all your fans."

He made a face. "There're a lot of guests," he said after a moment.

"It's a wedding. Of course there are a lot of guests."

"I overheard Gwen talking with Mrs. Ferth. There were a lot of guests added at the last minute."

Lady Gwendolyn Corbin was their mother's lady-in-waiting, and Mrs. Ferth the Queen's personal secretary. Naturally, the two women had been involved in the guest list. "Owen, it's a wedding. A royal wedding, planned in an excruciatingly brief amount of time. Who knows what details went into the guest list." Something in her brother's eyes made hers narrow humorously. "Imagining conspiracies?"

His lips twitched, as she knew they would. "Only of Mrs. Ferth trying to stack the room with suitable prospective missus Owens."

Meredith laughed softly. Owen would never be manipulated that way. Even at twenty-three, he was too much a man of his own. "Well, prospective brides aside, there are a number of pretty young things in the room who would be more than happy for ten minutes of your company. So what are you doing dancing with your old sister?"

"Because he wants to dance with his sister who isn't so old," Anastasia said behind her, and Meredith looked over her shoulder to see her little sister dancing with Colonel Prescott.

Meredith barely had time to suck in a surprised breath before Owen and Anastasia neatly maneuvered into switching partners. Which left Meredith—right there in the center of the ballroom, surrounded by other swaying couples—facing Pierce.

"Seems we've been here before," he said evenly, and held out his arms.

She needed no reminder of that long-ago spring ball when he'd not only refused a dance with her, but had told her to try her fledgling girlish wiles on someone who was interested.

Just tired enough, with just enough champagne in her system, Meredith completely ignored the dictates of good behavior. "No. I don't think so. I wouldn't want you to put yourself out." Her voice was cool. And when she turned on her high heel and slipped away through the crowd, she felt satisfaction. This time she'd turned him down flat.

At least that was what she told herself.

Only her satisfaction felt rather more painfully like disappointment.

Chapter Three

The last thing in the world Pierce expected was for Meredith to turn and run. The amusement that drifted through him wasn't at all appropriate.

Well, Meredith had always been full of surprises. Though she'd been a model daughter, she hadn't married in her early twenties when most thought she should have done so. She'd obtained advanced degrees at universities abroad and she'd taken the type of job that was ordinarily handled by a well-heeled staff member. She had her causes, certainly. But Meredith was, first and foremost, a professional woman. And Pierce didn't admit to many that he'd followed her career, as much with pride as with the intent of insuring her safety.

If he were smart, he'd take his leave. There really was no reason for Pierce to remain at the gala reception. There were other members of the RET around to keep a close eye on the matters that absolutely required their attention.

But Pierce was obviously not smart. Not tonight. Because he smoothly snagged a flute of champagne as a tray passed and he headed slowly, deliberately for the terrace. The two guards on either side of the door, already at attention, snapped even more so as he passed them, and he automatically returned the salute.

Young, he thought. Baby-faced soldiers who would, pray heaven, never be called upon to do things such as he'd done. Nor to see things such as he'd seen.

He held the grim thoughts close as he stepped onto the terrace, his eyes adjusting to the dark. There were strands of tiny white lights everywhere, making it look almost like a fairy tale. But the lights provided far less illumination than atmosphere.

Still, he saw her. Meredith. Standing alone, adrift in a swath of dull gold silk, her hands resting on the low stone wall at the perimeter of the terrace. Nothing glaring or flashy for Meredith. She was far too classic for that. The only time she glittered was when she wore a jeweled tiara or a collar of diamonds.

How many times had he heard his men talking about the three princesses fair? Meredith, Megan and Anastasia. There wasn't a man living in the country who hadn't fantasized about one of them at one time or another. Who hadn't dreamed of sharing a word or a dance or a kiss with any one of their Royal Highnesses.

Pierce rolled the crystal flute between his fingers

and wondered what she was thinking as she stood looking at the sea, her profile as pure as the cool moonlight that outlined it.

Was she thinking of Megan and Jean-Paul? Pierce knew the couple would be spending their honeymoon at sail. Or was there something else on Meredith's mind? *Someone* else?

Whatever thoughts circled in Meredith's head were none of his business, of course. None at all. Which didn't explain in the least why Pierce was allowing himself to dwell on it. He wasn't a masochist. And thinking about Meredith, knowing there wasn't one bloody thing he could do about the reasons he must remain uninvolved with her, did nothing but cause him pain.

Pierce's business was intelligence. Professionally, he'd kept more than his share of secrets. Some he'd created or caused, some he'd protected. Keeping his feelings for Meredith under control, under wraps, never to let them see the light of day, was about the most difficult secret he faced. When he was at the base, at the small home he'd inherited from his parents in the Aronleigh Mountains or even at his flat in Sterling, it wasn't such a daily struggle.

When in Marlestone, however, the capital city, with this very impressive palace looking over it, Pierce felt constantly battered with the desire to get closer to her and the need to remain away. Far away.

And everyone said women were contrary creatures, he thought ironically as he headed not safely toward the nearest exit and home but straight toward Meredith.

She didn't betray so much as a start when he joined

her at the low stone wall. A breeze had kicked up. Moonlight caught, trapped and gently released in the swelling ripples of water so far below.

"I love the scent," Meredith murmured.

"Sea."

"Yes."

"Your sister will have a good life with Jean-Paul. He's a good man."

Her chin tilted slightly, and he caught the gleam of the sideways glance she gave him. "Don't read my mind, Colonel. It isn't polite."

"I'm not often accused of being polite."

"Please. You are beyond polite, and we both know it."

The thoughts circling in his head weren't in the same universe as polite. "Why did you blow off George earlier? He looked a broken man when you came out here."

"Why did you tear yourself away from Juliet's charms?"

"Obvious as they are," he added smoothly.

She let out a short, breathy laugh that sent a charge straight down his spine. In defense, he lifted his champagne glass and drank. Given a choice, he'd far prefer beer. "Are you avoiding the answer?" Holding onto the glass, he balanced it on the wall.

"George is a very nice man," she said smoothly. "Why are you here, Colonel?"

"The music inside was giving me a headache, and I wanted a smoke."

"You don't smoke."

"How do you know?"

"Because I remember when you quit."

"Oh, yes. During the memorable summer of your tenth year when you were busy surrounding yourself with your royal attitude."

"The memorable summer of *your* seventeenth," she countered. "When you were busy surrounding yourself with teenage girls endowed with charms easily as obvious as dear Juliet's."

Did he detect pique in her tone? He drank a little more champagne, figuring it was wishful thinking on his part.

"So, I don't smoke," he admitted. He had, briefly, but his poor mother had been so scandalized, he hadn't had the heart to keep up the habit.

Again, he caught that sidelong look from her. He wondered if she knew the effect that kind of look had on a man. Probably. She was smooth, intelligent and well past the age of consent. Which did not mean that standing there in the moonlight with her was not one of the most foolish indulgences ever.

She finished her champagne and turned a little. Facing him. "Truthfully, I was standing here thinking about something Owen said. About all the unfamiliar faces here."

Pierce had noticed that, as well. And done his share of wondering. Speculating. Though it was a royal wedding, it was not a state occasion, and the guest list had not gone through some of the channels it otherwise would have. He hadn't seen the list himself until last week when it was submitted to Royal Intelligence. At that point, his men and women had kicked their diligence into high gear to insure the safety of everyone who came to the wedding.

It was what they did. Protecting Penwyck, its citizens, its interests, its ruling house.

It's what Pierce did, as well. And had been doing for more of his life than not. More than that, it was what he *was*.

"Your new brother-in-law contributed to the guest list," he said. "As did his parents and uncle, undoubtedly. The King and Queen had their lists, as well. Guests they wanted to include for whatever reason. Not every face would be recognizable under those circumstances."

"And you're one of them. Well—" she lifted a slender, long-fingered hand "—you're not unfamiliar, but you're certainly not a face we often see at the palace."

"It's an important event."

"The other events in which we are involved are not?"

"We?"

She gestured gracefully. "We. The family. You *do* tend to avoid us, you know. Why is that, I wonder?"

He was, first and foremost, a military man. Yet he'd walked blindly into that mine field. Diversion, he thought. "Dance with me."

Her lips parted softly. "I believe we covered that."

"Not exactly." He left his glass on the wide ledge next to hers and took her hand. It was undoubtedly only surprise that let her step so easily away from the stone wall and into his arms. The music was softer out here. Still audible. But it was barely a background to the sound of the breeze through the leaves of the trees surrounding the estate, the distant lap of the sea against Castle Cove. And the music was fairly inau-

dible when his senses were suddenly, achingly aware
of the cadence of Meredith's breath, the soft scrape
of shoe against stone and brick as they swayed.

"You're trembling."

"It's chilly out here with the breeze."

She lied, he thought. It was a balmy, breezy night.
And he was burning up, holding her. Though there
was more space between them than decorum demanded. His fingers barely grazed the fabric covering
the small of her back, and her fingertips barely
touched his shoulder. Where their other hands linked,
however, a flame burned between their palms. Hot.
Enticing.

Impossible.

"You ought to go inside," he said. "If you're
chilly."

"Yes."

Yet she made no move to do so. In fact, as one
song melded into the next, the distance between them
lessened. Until Pierce eventually realized that his
arms were definitely full of warm, sweet-smelling
woman. That they'd shuffled and swayed themselves
into the rear corner of the terrace. Where light barely
reached, where the salty scent of sea was nearly a
tang on their lips.

Her hair smelled of orange blossoms, he thought,
and he felt like a drowning man. His palm flattened
against her spine, and he felt her long, slow intake of
breath that pressed her breasts against his chest. Her
hand glided, measuring, over his shoulder to his collar. Her fingertips grazed his neck below his ear. His
nape. Her forehead found the perfect resting place
below his jaw. Heart to heart. Curve to angle.

She was royal by birth. She was the daughter of his King.

He had no business holding her the way he was. No business wanting to imprint his body on hers and hers on his. Not with the secrets he was keeping from her.

"Mer—Your Royal Highness." His jaw was aching again. Hell. Every part of him ached.

"Would you mind?" She leaned back, swaying a little. Making him wonder, all of a sudden, just how much champagne she'd consumed. "My shoes. They're so tight."

A moment later, she was several inches shorter. Obviously, she'd stepped out of her high heels. And she'd kicked them with her foot until they tumbled against each other, stopped only by the wall.

It wasn't his shoes that were tight, he thought with grim humor as she linked her hands behind his neck and nestled against him. "That's better," she sighed, sounding tired. "You dance well, Colonel."

He was doing little other than holding her against him. "You should go to bed."

Her lashes lifted, and she looked at him. He wished there were more illumination so he could tell if her eyes were glazed with champagne or drowsy with desire. Either was inappropriate to take advantage of, and he knew it.

"I don't think I'm the spoiled brat I was at ten. Or seventeen," she said, lucidly enough, "who needs to be sent to bed."

At seventeen, she'd been a burgeoning young woman, just beginning to grasp the feminine power she could wield over others. A power that was now in full bloom.

Apparently, though he was nearly at a standstill, she, without her too-tight shoes, felt rather more like dancing. Swaying hypnotically. He clamped his hands on her waist. Her hips. She was tormenting him, and she probably didn't even know it. Despite his torment, he knew there were guests inside the ballroom who were dancing far more closely, far more uninhibitedly.

"You weren't a brat," he said.

"But I was spoiled."

"You're the beloved first child of our ruler."

"Spoken very properly." She tossed back her head and watched him from beneath her lashes. "Do you ever lose your composure, Colonel Prescott?"

Only with you. Her lips looked impossibly soft. Inviting. "Rarely," he said. "Do you ever fail to get what you want?"

"Rarely. So, if I'm not the spoiled brat, then why do you feel compelled to send me off to bed as if I were?"

Holding Meredith against him while speaking about bed hadn't been particularly wise of him. His imagination was running riot. "Simple concern for your welfare, Your Royal Highness. You've had a long day. And plenty of champagne, I think."

She smiled beautifully, telling him more surely than ever that she had imbibed more than was usual. As far as Pierce knew, Meredith never drank to excess. She never did a single thing to cause her family worry.

"Haven't you had a long day, as well? Weren't

you up before dawn for your run in the hills around the base? Or in your old age have you given up your three morning miles?''

Old age? There were times when thirty-five felt old. There were times, like now, with a beautiful woman against him that were something else entirely. ''Five miles. At the park near my place in Sterling.''

''That's right.'' She nodded thoughtfully. ''I'd heard you'd taken a flat there. A few years ago.'' She shot him another one of those veiled looks. ''What brought that about, anyway? No, wait. A woman, I'll wager.''

''Yes.''

Her eyebrows rose a little. ''And that's all you have to say about it, I suppose.''

''Yes.''

''Closemouthed as always, Colonel Prescott. Intelligence really is right up your alley.''

''I took the flat because I was driving my men and women crazy being on base twenty-four seven.'' He'd be hanged if he'd admit to Meredith that *she* was the reason he'd chosen Sterling. It was a large city. Larger than Marlestone. And it was far enough away from Marlestone that he'd be unlikely to run into Meredith.

''Thinking only of others, as usual,'' Meredith murmured, then quickly hid a yawn behind her hand. ''Heavens. Please excuse me.''

''I'm surprised you even heard about my place in Sterling.'' Or that she remembered his penchant for running in the morning—a hangover from the days he'd run track in school. ''It's hardly the stuff for the gossips.''

"You're eligible, attractive and the Duke of Aron-leigh. Surely you don't expect to be immune from the paparazzi?"

"I'm a colonel in the Penwyck army," he said flatly.

Her eyebrows shot up. "Did I hit a nerve?"

He consciously relaxed his grip on her slender waist. "You should get back inside."

"Why?"

"Because we've been out here for some time now."

"Afraid it'll mar your reputation as the immovable, untouchable colonel?"

"I'm afraid George Valdosta will fall to the ground, prostrate in grief that you're out of sight, and he'll be trampled to death by dancers."

"It always surprises me that you've a sense of hu-mor lurking beneath your stony exterior, Colonel Prescott."

She didn't have a clue what lurked beneath his ex-terior. It was just as well. "Gossip aside, the papers tomorrow morning will be filled with accounts of the wedding."

"This morning," she corrected. "It's past mid-night."

"And the princess really should be in bed."

"I'm not eight, Colonel. I'm twenty-eight." She was amused. Amused and drowsy and nearly boneless against him. "What is this preoccupation you have with my sleep habits?"

"Only your welfare."

She shook her head slightly, then tilted it to look

at him. "My father has always said you are a man of honor."

That was debatable, Pierce thought. Where was honor when the only reason he was out on this terrace with Meredith was that he didn't seem to have the fortitude to tear himself away?

"The speeches were lovely, don't you think?"

"Speeches?"

"During the dinner. I thought my mother would nearly faint when the King toasted the memory of my uncle. They didn't like one another much, you know."

She was scrambling his brains. "His Majesty and Edwin?"

"Yes."

His fingers flexed against her waist. Felt the seductive flare of her hips beneath the silk that wrapped her torso snugly, only to flare out in luxurious folds around her knees. "Edwin seems on your mind today."

She lifted her shoulder, drawing his bedeviled gaze to the ivory skin left bare to the moonlight. "He seemed on the minds of many," she said easily. "Isn't that what families do when they gather together for weddings and christenings and funerals and such? Talk about the rest of the family? Those present and those lost?"

"Your family is a far cry from the typical."

"Typical or not, I thought the toast was nice."

"For the Queen's sake," Pierce agreed.

Her head tilted again, this time brushing against the arm he'd slid behind her shoulders. Was it his imagination that she was looking at his mouth? "Did you know," she said softly, "that you get this hard look around your mouth whenever you say my uncle's name?"

"No."

"At least you don't deny it," she said.

"As I have no mirror on hand to test your theory, I'll have to take your word for it."

"'Tis more than a theory, Colonel." Her fingers flitted over his jaw. His cheek. "Right there," she whispered. "You get this fierce-looking crease in your cheek. Why is that?"

He caught her fingers in his, pulling them from his face. He didn't want Meredith pressing her lovely, aristocratic nose into his feelings, or lack of them, regarding Edwin.

Her fingers flexed against his, and he settled her hand safely on his shoulder once more. "So proper," she murmured.

If she only knew. "I'll take you inside."

She sighed faintly. "Of course." She turned away, and only through sheer will did he let go of her as if nothing untoward had been running through his mind. "Oh. My shoes." She looked at the ground where it was black as pitch.

Pierce knelt and felt around for the shoes until he found them. "Give me your foot."

"What every woman dreams of hearing," she murmured. But he heard the rustle of silk and tormented himself with images of her lifting it.

Then her foot butted his thigh. "Sorry," she said on a soft laugh.

"Admit it. You've wanted to kick me since you were ten."

She giggled.

Definitely too much champagne, he thought as he reached for her foot. Slowly slid the shoe into place. Her ankle felt delicate. Narrow.

"Are you certain that isn't a glass slipper there?"

He took his hand away from her ankle, aware that his hold was too lingering, and rapidly slid the other shoe on for her. "You've no need for fairy godmothers or glass slippers. You're already a princess."

"One without a prince," she said. Then laughed lightly, as if her voice hadn't sounded utterly melancholy. "Thank you for playing shoe man, Colonel. I'll just have to give away this pair, I think. Beautiful as they are, they've been torturing my toes the entire day."

"Your Royal Highness."

She turned on her heel so abruptly she swayed, and he put a steadying hand on her back. Was she as startled by the appearance of Lady Gwendolyn behind her as he'd been?

"Yes?"

"Your father is asking for you."

Meredith nodded. "Of course. Thank you." She looked over her shoulder at Pierce. "Colonel. The dance was…delightful. If I don't see you before you leave, I hope you'll have a safe trip home."

"Thank you."

With a sweep of her skirt, Meredith glided toward the terrace doors. As she neared, the light haloed around her, glinting off her hair, her dress, her ivory skin.

Pierce was glad for the relative darkness in which he stood. Lady Gwendolyn studied him silently for a moment. It had been a lot of years since he'd gone to Gwendolyn Corbin on the occasion of her husband's funeral to express his condolences at her loss, only to end up having to lie to the young woman when—tears flooding her lovely blue eyes—she'd asked him the most natural of questions. What her husband's last words had been.

Pierce still felt awkward in her presence.

The woman, with no smile whatsoever on her classically beautiful face, nodded briefly. "Good night, Your Grace." Then she turned and glided away.

Pierce turned around and stared over the wall into the night, his hands tight on the stone ledge. He hated the noble title.

There was nothing noble about him. Nothing at all.

He stood there, drawing in the increasingly crisp, sea-scented air, until his tension abated. Until he could be sure he wouldn't betray himself when he went into the ballroom. Only then did he turn and follow the women's path inside.

He immediately noticed Meredith in conversation with her father. She was smiling as she greeted the people in the group surrounding the King, but Pierce could see how tired she was.

If King Morgan were any kind of father, he'd have seen it, too. But the man standing beside Meredith wasn't any type of father. Not to Meredith. Nor to anyone else.

Because the man standing beside Meredith, foisting her off into dancing with one of the men, was not her father, King Morgan of Penwyck.

It was Morgan's twin brother, Broderick.

And Pierce was one of a very small handful of people in the country who knew it.

Chapter Four

As he circled the grand ballroom, Pierce's attention kept straying to Meredith. She was being passed from one gentleman to the next, barely managing two minutes of dance between the lot of them.

His hands curled. It was nearing two in the morning. She was tipsy on champagne and nerves. It was none of his business with whom she danced away the hours.

She'd always been out of his reach. Never more so than now.

Even the King's family didn't know about the health crisis that had necessitated bringing in Broderick to act as king.

And it was *that* secret, right now, that ate most at Pierce's conscience. He wanted to go onto that dance floor and rescue Meredith with her aching feet and her tired body from the demands of her position in the royal family.

But she *was* out of his reach. She always had been. She always would be. Instead of heading toward the exit, Pierce headed toward the King. He was aware of the cold expression in Broderick's eyes as he joined the small group of men cloistered around him. But he didn't let Broderick's expression stop him.

"Your Majesty," he greeted respectfully. "Could we have a word?"

Broderick's lips thinned. He waved off his crowd and, though nobody saw the reluctance but Pierce, walked with him to the terrace, then into the rose garden, passing the guard who quietly assured Pierce that the area was secure. "Spending a lot of time out of doors, Prescott," Broderick said smoothly. "Is the moon full?"

"If you're implying I'm a wolf under this tux, you'd be right." Pierce didn't like Broderick. He liked lying about this business even less. It wasn't the first lie he'd kept secret from the rest of the royal family, but this one sat more heavily on his conscience than the other.

Probably because he was worried about the true King.

Morgan should have come out of his coma by now, yet he hadn't. And the doctors who were privy to the truth were noticeably concerned. They were even now covertly consulting the Centers for Disease Control in the United States. Megan's bout with encephalitis had resolved extremely rapidly. The King's case, however, seemed another kettle of fish entirely.

Lies, Pierce thought as he watched Broderick pluck a fat bloom from a laden rosebush. He hated lies.

The last situation had been unavoidable, and even ten years later, Pierce knew he'd undoubtedly take the same actions. Now, however, this game of make-believe could make or break the delicate negotiations involved in the alliances that King Morgan had been so determined to see to fruition.

"Did you add to the guest list?" he finally asked.

Broderick barely spared him a look. "My dear Prescott, is that not the right of any father of the bride?"

"Don't mess with me, sir."

Broderick turned on Pierce, smiling coldly. And in that coldness, his startling resemblance to his twin brother was lost. "And don't mess with me, old boy. I didn't have to agree to this charade of yours, after all. The high and mighty RET. My brother's pet team. I could have told you all to go to hell."

The Royal Elite Team was far more than the King's pet, and Broderick knew it. They were a group of four men, personally selected by King Morgan, to protect and serve every interest of Penwyck. If there were a modern-day musketeer, Pierce figured his associates of the RET and he would be it. Though their efforts these days rarely involved wielding the sword themselves.

He didn't rise to Broderick's taunt. "You could have refused. You didn't."

"It's to Penwyck's advantage that I was able to step into my sainted brother's shoes," Broderick said. His fingers slowly plucked the petals from the rose.

"We didn't expect the charade to have to continue

beyond a few days. A week.'' Nobody had expected the King to be indisposed for so long a time. It had them all worried.

Broderick nodded slowly, for once exhibiting a small portion of concern. ''Yet my brother hasn't rallied as expected. A terrible thing. Lying there in a coma. The man didn't even have an opportunity to name his successor. To choose between his twin sons the way my parents had to choose between Morgan and me.''

And you hated your parents for the choice they made, didn't you, old boy? Pierce kept the thought to himself. Broderick had been living in relative seclusion on Majorco, thoroughly estranged from his brother, for so many years that few people even remembered his existence, but he had to admit that, so far, Broderick had been doing an admirable job of taking his brother's place.

None of which mitigated Pierce's concern for the King, who lay in that damnably prolonged coma, secreted from all but the most necessary and trusted of staff.

And whether or not Pierce liked it, Broderick was a member of the royal family. ''Your Royal Highness—''

''Majesty,'' Broderick snapped. ''You will address me as you address the King, or you will not address me at all. Is that clear?''

Pierce stepped close to the King, keeping his voice low. ''And you will not overstep yourself so much as an inch, or *we* will deal appropriately with you. Is that clear?''

Broderick suddenly smiled and stepped back,

breaking the tension between them. "Relax, Prescott. I swear, neither you nor Monteque have any idea how to have fun. The good admiral dogged my footsteps for most of the night before he was—hallelujah—called away."

Admiral Harrison Monteque was the unofficial leader of the four-man Royal Elite Team. And Pierce knew Harrison was about as trusting of Broderick as he was. "Adding guests that were never run by my team is hardly what I'd describe as having fun. Yet that's what you did, isn't it?"

Broderick shrugged. "So, I was having a bit of fun at the family's expense. Everyone loves a party, Prescott. What's a few dozen people more or less?"

"It's a few dozen people who haven't been run through security," Pierce said flatly. "There is no excuse for putting any member of the Penwycks at risk, yet you did just that."

Broderick sighed heavily. "All right. All right. Relax. Everyone is safe and my...friends have nearly all departed."

There was little Pierce could do about it without tipping his hand, and Broderick knew that. "How are things going in the private quarters? Anyone suspicious?" If Meredith had noticed anything amiss, he probably would have known by now. She was nothing if not excruciatingly honest.

He wished he were the kind of man who could be just as candid. Who could be worthy of a woman like her. But he wasn't.

He hadn't been for ten long years.

"Not even the Queen herself when I slipped into her bed last night has shown suspicion."

Pierce's stomach twisted, and his hands curled into fists. "You gave your word you would not—"

"Relax. You have no sense of humor, Prescott."

"Not when it comes to the safety of the King or his family," Pierce agreed flatly.

Broderick tossed aside the ruined rose. "My brother is fool enough to have separate chambers from his beautiful wife. As I'm walking in his shoes, it appears I must be the fool, as well. Now, is that all you came to discuss? To chastise me for adding a few unimportant guests?"

Pierce watched Broderick through narrowed eyes. He hated the fact that the charade had gone on this long. He particularly hated the fact that, as it had gone on this long, telling the Queen the truth had become a delicate problem. The woman would rightfully be appalled at what had been kept from her.

"Don't forget the meeting tomorrow morning with Cole Everson and Admiral Monteque," he said.

"It's on my schedule," Broderick assured smoothly.

Still, Pierce didn't trust him. Only one other time had Broderick come through for his twin brother. But that time had saved too many lives to be discounted, so Pierce and the rest of the RET were banking on that speck of familial loyalty to continue reigning within the black sheep of the Penwyck clan. "We'll be going over some points in the signing of the alliances," he said.

"Yes, yes." Clearly bored with the subject, Broderick started toward the ballroom. As soon as he passed the silent guard, Pierce knew he'd have to treat the man with all the respect due the King.

It stuck in his craw, having to do so.

King Morgan was deserving of every bit of respect he was shown. He'd earned it through his vision, his dedication, his love for his country and its people.

Broderick had earned nothing.

But he was doing them a favor, at least until the alliances so desired by King Morgan were a fact and not a dream, and it was incumbent upon Pierce to continue the odd dance in which the RET and Broderick were engaged. The one thing King Morgan had been determined to accomplish was the signing of the alliances. If the King were temporarily incapacitated, then the RET would accomplish it in the King's stead. It was that simple.

And that complicated, Pierce thought grimly, as he followed Broderick into the ballroom where Meredith was still dancing and chatting and generally acting the gracious hostess. Anastasia and Owen were nowhere in sight, and when he asked, he learned they'd retired.

There was no basis for his reluctance to leave Meredith there. The guards were still at their posts. It may well have been heading toward dawn, but until the last guest departed or was ensconced in one of the guest rooms of the palace, the guards would remain.

Nevertheless, Pierce hung around for a while longer, sipping a coffee he'd finagled from one of the maids, and wondered how on God's green earth people could party for so long, so late. George Valdosta, Pierce noticed, was slumped in a chair, a squat tumbler of liquor in front of him. His eyes never left Meredith.

Pierce felt a small measure of sympathy for the

man. It was all he could do to keep from openly staring at her.

Another hour slowly ticked by. Guests departed. The King retired. The band, the third one of the night, had settled into one long bluesy run after another. Heavy on bass and moaning sax, it seemed fitting for the late hour when the few remaining couples clung to each other on the dance floor, barely making any attempt at dancing.

No different than the kind of dancing he and Meredith had done on the terrace, he thought with dark humor.

Meredith was still on her feet. Surrounded, typically.

Pierce wondered how anyone could not see the weariness in her face. He wondered how she kept on. But then, she was a Penwyck. And the family was notorious for always continuing.

He was on his third cup of coffee when she finally extricated herself from the persistent guests. She walked by where he sat among a trio of decorative potted trees, then stopped and turned. "You're still here."

"You're still playing hostess." She looked like perfection, but he could see her underlying pallor. The woman was exhausted. She had been for several hours. Of course it was worse now.

"Someone needs to play hostess, don't you think?"

"I think the people who are still here show remarkably poor manners."

"You're still here."

"As I said." He smiled faintly and drained the rest

of the coffee from his cup. It had long gone cold. "Tell the band to stop wailing, and the hangers-on will get the message quickly enough."

She tilted her head a little, her clear green eyes curious. "Why *are* you still here, Colonel?"

"Because you're still playing hostess." He attributed his blunt honesty to the absurdly late hour. Better that than the fact that he'd been watching every male who came within her vicinity with some sort of caged antagonism. He hardly liked admitting it to himself.

She moistened her lips, seeming to absorb that. If she'd been tipsy earlier, now she seemed stone sober. "As it happens, I was taking my leave. Satisfied?"

Hardly. "Yes."

She smiled faintly. "Well, then. It was nice of you to share the occasion with us, Colonel."

He rose, and she smoothly took a step back. Putting distance between them. "Is that what you've been telling everyone in the room?"

"As a matter of fact, yes." Her lips were a little less soft looking. "Good night, Colonel. Have a safe trip home." She started for the rear corner of the ballroom where Pierce knew there was a nearly invisible door that led to an enclosed walkway from the public buildings to the private family quarters. But she stopped short and headed instead for one of the terrace doors.

Pierce's gaze drifted over George, who'd been on the pathway to the interior exit. When Meredith took the other route, disappearing outside, George popped up like an eager marionette and hurried after her. With no particular reason other than annoyance with the other man for not giving it a rest, Pierce followed George.

They were a regular parade.

Well beyond the drift of the blues band, Pierce could easily hear the click of Meredith's heels against the footpath leading toward the formal gardens. He heard the low timbre of George's voice. And then silence.

The back of his neck prickled, and he soundlessly continued forward. Rounding the yew maze in just enough time to see Meredith tugging her arm from George's grip. In just enough time to see George grab her again, quickly, trying to pull her closer.

Meredith wanted to laugh at the ridiculousness of the situation. Laugh, or kick George Valdosta in the leg. She wriggled away from him. ''George, you've had too much to drink.''

Not so much that his rapid hands were slowed in the least, however, and her twisted sense of humor fled when his hands clamped on her arms. Too tight. Too eager. Too forward, as she had no desire whatsoever to have her arms clamped upon by George Valdosta regardless of how long they'd known one another. She pulled back as he pulled forward, and she was seriously considering that hard kick when she heard the scrape of a shoe. And a voice from the shadows near the maze.

''Darling, I got here as quickly as I could. Hullo, George. Better see to your car,'' he suggested. ''The guards are getting ready to secure the gates for the night.''

She managed to keep her jaw from hanging, just, as Pierce strolled into the dim light afforded by the late moon. George's hands fell away in the moment before Pierce closed his, warm and steady, over her shoulders and drew her against him, heading toward the private quarters as if he'd been doing it every day of his adult life.

Meredith looked over his shoulder to see George walking away, his shoulders slumped in dejection.

"I can get him back for you, if you like," Pierce said smoothly.

She looked forward. "No, thank you," she said faintly. "Were you following us?"

"He was following you. I was following him."

The guilty pleasure she felt quickly deflated. "I see."

She heard his soft snort. "I doubt it." He continued walking her to a side door that would let her into the reception area of the private quarters. His arm slid from her shoulder, and he opened the door for her, standing aside.

Telling herself she did *not* feel chilled without his arm about her, she looked into his face. Such a familiar face, and still such a stranger to her. "Thank you for, well, for protecting me."

He didn't respond to that. "Good night, Your Royal Highness."

Familiar face. Familiar distance, she thought with a faint sigh. As if they had never danced hip to hip, breast to breast, beneath the moonlight.

She stepped through the door. "Good night, Colonel."

Chapter Five

"Darling, please. You're not so late that you can't sit and have some tea."

Meredith paused in the doorway of the breakfast room. She'd overslept. She was already late for work. And she couldn't abide tardiness. "Mother, really. I've got to go."

The Queen, perfectly coiffed and dressed for the day in a beautiful ivory suit that set off her dark hair, smiled serenely. "Of course, darling. Have a good day."

Meredith's shoulders very nearly slumped. She set her briefcase and purse on an empty chair and grabbed a china saucer and cup, filling it with tea. "Has Owen already raced through here?"

"He was heading out as I was sitting down. I don't believe he'd even been to sleep."

Meredith hid a smile at her brother's antics. "Have you had any word from Dylan?"

"No. I'm certain he's out there having the time of his life clambering up the sides of mountains and goodness knows what else. He'll come home when he's ready."

"And you already miss Megan." Meredith sat beside her mother.

Marissa smiled faintly. "She's my daughter. Of course I miss her. I'll miss you, too, when you marry and go off to live your life."

An image of Pierceson Prescott flashed in Meredith's mind, and she ducked her head over the teacup. All she succeeded in doing was scorching her tongue on the piping hot liquid. The colonel's image was firmly stuck in her mind. "I think you needn't worry about that happening any time soon," she murmured. "It's not as if I have suitors lining up with marriage proposals." Propositions, perhaps, like the unexpected one George Valdosta had had the inebriated audacity to voice the previous night.

"Only because you hold them off, darling."

"Mother—"

"All right." Marissa lifted a graceful hand. "I shan't complain too much. After all, Megan and Jean-Paul are giving me a start on the grandchildren I've been longing for. Granny Marissa. It has a nice sound, don't you think?"

Meredith snorted softly. If ever there was a woman who did not fit the granny image, it was the Queen of Penwyck. Marissa was only fifty-three years old and looked a solid ten younger than that, to boot.

"I wasn't aware you were so anxious to have

grandchildren.'' Especially given the Queen and King's stunned reaction to Megan's unexpected pregnancy, Meredith thought.

"Of course I want grandchildren. More than that, though, I'd like to see my children happily married.'' Marissa gently patted Meredith's hand where it rested on the linen-covered table. "Actually, Gwen tells me that, though Anastasia shared a dance with Colonel Prescott, it was *you* he was looking rather cozy with on the terrace last evening.''

Meredith flushed. She should have known her mother's dearest friend would tell her about that. "We *were* sharing a dance.''

"Of course, dear.''

Her cheeks felt even hotter. "That's *all* it was.''

"Yes.'' Marissa, utterly unperturbed by her daughter's consternation, tilted the teapot over her cup, topping off the perfect brew. "A simple dance. Nothing more. I understand completely.'' She dribbled a small amount of milk in her cup, gave one swirl with a silver spoon and set the spoon smoothly on the saucer.

Her mother's tea routine never changed, Meredith thought, vaguely soothed by the normalcy of it.

Her soothed senses were jogged when her mother said blandly, "Colonel Prescott cuts quite a figure in his uniform, doesn't he.''

"Mother!''

Marissa smiled, her eyes glinting with a mischief reserved only for her children. "Well? I do have eyes, darling.''

"Yes, you do. Eyes of the most beautiful robin's egg blue,'' a voice said from the door.

Both women turned, looking with surprise at the

King who was standing there with a faint smile on his handsome face.

"Morgan." Marissa rose to fetch a cup and saucer from the sideboard. "I thought you'd already gone this morning."

The King sauntered into the room, his hazel eyes lingering on Marissa as she handed him his tea. "I thought I'd have breakfast with my wife." He brushed his thumb down Marissa's smooth cheek in a decidedly lingering way.

Meredith stared hard into her cup. It was better than staring hard at her father. There was no doubt in her mind that her father and mother loved each other despite the fact that their marriage had been an arranged one. Yet visible displays of affection, even within the privacy of the family and the confines of their residence, were few and far between.

The caress seemed to fluster Marissa, as well, Meredith noted. She might be twenty-eight years old, but she absolutely was not accustomed to seeing her father flirt with her mother. She just wasn't. It was, well, embarrassing. Which made her feel all of ten years old again when she'd first learned the facts of life. "I've got to run," she announced brightly.

"You didn't eat a thing." Her mother turned toward her, chiding. A queen she may be, but she still fussed over her brood.

To satisfy Marissa, Meredith grabbed a piece of toast from the basket on the table and tucked it between her teeth as she gathered her briefcase and purse.

"Meredith." The King shook his head slightly and sat at the head of the table. "Really."

With her hands free again, she removed the toast from her mouth. "I've got to run by Penwyck Memorial to pick up some stuff for the children's center opening."

"See you at dinner?"

"Of course." Meredith smiled at her mother, though it felt a little forced. Where else would she be? She hadn't had cause to have dinner out in ages unless it was for some official function.

Then, disgusted with her wave of self-pity, she hurried out to the drive where her car was waiting. Pitching her handfuls onto the seat beside her, she slid into the little roadster and set off with a roar of the engine.

Oh, she really did loathe being late.

The thought was still circling in her head an hour later when she finally sailed through the secured entrance of the Royal Intelligence Institute.

The sight of her secretary sitting behind the reception desk brought her up short. "Lillian, how many years of newspapers do we have on record?"

"Two years on paper. Twenty on microfilm."

Meredith nodded. Perfect. Juggling the strap of her briefcase and her narrow envelope purse, she stopped at the coffee stand and filled her cup, overflowing it on the first try and burning her thumb.

Lillian half jumped from her post at Meredith's gasp. "Are you all right?"

Meredith waved her back. Her mind still seemed to be barely firing, and she had a vicious headache. "Just clumsy. I hate being late."

"I hardly think anyone will fire you for a few minutes," Lillian said dryly.

Meredith smiled. Lillian was correct, of course. No

one at the Royal Intelligence Institute would dream of commenting over her tardiness. But Meredith took pride in being well qualified for her position. She took pride in doing well.

Which did not include strolling into the office forty-seven minutes late. She should probably have given tea with her mother a miss. That would have shaved off about ten minutes, at least.

"Is there something you'd like me to retrieve for you?"

Meredith dragged her thoughts together with an effort. The newspapers. "Oh, no, Lillian. I can do it. Just something I'm sort of curious about."

"You're certain it isn't *this* you're curious about?" Lillian held out her issue of that day's paper. The front page was consumed with coverage of Megan's wedding. A dozen photos, at least, followed the headlines, many of them not focused on the bridal couple at all.

Anastasia and Owen commandeered their share of pictures, and Meredith—well, Meredith was caught boldly in the act of kissing Pierceson Prescott during the wedding ceremony. Next to that damning photo was a long-distance shot of her standing on the terrace alongside him, their hands very nearly touching atop the stone ledge. The captions beneath the pair of photos speculated whether the eldest princess was contemplating romance with the elusive Duke of Aronleigh.

"Darned long-distance lenses," Meredith murmured, and tucked the newspaper in her briefcase. She was used to seeing her photograph in newspapers. Whether she liked it or not, it was part and parcel of who she was. But on top of her mother's comments earlier, it seemed harder to take than usual. And what idiot had allowed cameras to be part of the wedding ceremony, anyway? Was nothing sacred anymore?

She realized her secretary was watching her curiously. "I want to look up the accounts of my uncle's death," she admitted, scrambling for composure.

"Something in particular you're looking for?"

"No." Meredith smiled at the woman and turned to head up the corridor to the left of reception. "Nothing in particular." Technically, Lillian was Meredith's secretary, and she could easily have been put on the little project. But it was only Meredith's curiosity that was spurring on the interest, and it seemed silly to have one of the staff devote their work time to it. Aside from which, Lillian already had extra duties on her plate as she had been filling in for the regular receptionist who was away on honeymoon.

Everyone seemed to be marrying, lately.

The thought snuck in, adding to the throb in Meredith's temples. She stopped and turned. "Have we received any more RSVPs for the Horizons event?"

The woman nodded, reaching for the subtly buzzing telephone as she held out a computerized list. "The latest," she mouthed before greeting the telephone caller.

Meredith took the list and hurried on her way. Her briefcase flapped against her hip, and her purse strap was slipping from her shoulder, making her wish she'd gone to her office before getting the coffee.

She rounded the last corner toward her office and nearly skidded to a halt at the surprising sight of Pierce, Admiral Harrison Monteque of the royal navy and Cole Everson, who was head of the RII, leaving Cole's office and heading straight toward her.

Neither Harrison nor Cole gave Meredith so much as a glance as they neared.

Her office was at one end of the hall, Cole's at the other. The colonel, however, looked at her without seeming to take his attention from his companions in the least.

That one look, brief though it was, made Meredith want to smooth a nervous hand over her hair. To tug at the hem of her suit jacket. To fuss with her appearance in the way women for centuries had fussed when certain men looked their way.

Fortunately, her hands were already too full, so she couldn't embarrass herself any more than necessary. She juggled her briefcase and her purse and managed to unlock her office door.

But then the trio passed beside her. And she had to turn to face them. She greeted Cole and the admiral, who both nodded politely, if rather absently, as they continued on their way.

And Pierce, well, Pierce looked her right in the eye and wished her a good morning. Then he caught the weight of her briefcase before she managed to spill her coffee right down the front of her suit. "You need another hand," he said.

What she needed was her head examined. Because the pleasure sweeping through her at seeing him was completely insane.

The colonel followed her through the doorway, and her spacious office suddenly felt confining. He set her briefcase on the corner of her pristine, glass-topped desk. She murmured her thanks, fully expecting him to take his leave. She could hear the other men's voices carrying as they headed down the corridor.

But Pierce didn't leave. "Nice office," he said, looking around.

She set her coffee cup on the desk with only a small rattle. Her office was identical to at least a dozen others in the complex. The only difference being that she'd brought in her own decorator for her office. And she'd paid for it out of her own pocket. Something that she'd often felt compelled to point out when some individuals commented on her supposed special treatment. "Thank you." She sat in her desk chair and, feeling more herself, looked at the Colonel.

He had fresh lines fanning from the corners of his eyes, she thought. Impossibly attractive. Yet she could tell he was as tired as she felt.

"What brings you to the RII?"

"A meeting."

"I sort of gathered that," she said dryly. She didn't take offense at the inscrutable answer. The RII was often involved in highly classified projects. Unless it directly involved the royal family, she was perfectly content in being left out of those numerous loops.

"How is your head?"

She felt her cheeks heat and cursed her fair skin. "Pained," she admitted ruefully. "It's the bubbles, I've decided. Sparkling wine always gives me a headache."

"Ought to stick to the unbubbled kind."

Lillian entered the room, and Meredith abruptly realized she was leaning on her arms toward him across the desk, smiling broadly. She hastily sat back, adjusting her expression.

Lillian looked at Pierce. "Pardon my interruption, Your Grace," she said, looking a little flustered at finding him in Meredith's office. She turned quickly to Meredith and handed her a small cartridge. "I pulled the film from ten years ago," she said efficiently.

Meredith thanked her and set the tape aside, barely noticing when her secretary left just as quickly and quietly as she'd entered.

"What's interesting about ten years ago?"

Meredith dragged her eyes from the very excellent cut of Pierce's khaki uniform. Or, more likely, the very excellent cut of the man beneath the uniform. It was no wonder Lillian had been a little flustered. Pierce-

son Prescott could have that affect on anyone. "My uncle's death," she said absently. Did she know anyone who looked as good in a uniform as did Pierce?

"Why?"

She focused a little. Picked up the microfilm cartridge and turned it over in her fingers. "Well, actually, it was something you said yesterday."

"Me?" He looked disbelieving.

"You know. About how I must have hardly known the man and all that. And truthfully, I don't know the details of my uncle's death. Not really. I'd just gone away for university. I know as much about Penwyck's place in the world—economically, politically and socially—as it is possible to know, but when it comes to my own family…" She shrugged.

"Ask your father."

"I will. If I feel the need. But I'd just as soon not trouble him with questions while he's so consumed with the alliances. And I don't necessarily want to ask my mother. I don't want to bring back bad memories for her. I'd just like to understand better what occurred. I feel as if I should know more. Does that make sense?''

He made a noncommittal sound.

Well, no matter. She would do what she wanted whether it made sense to anyone else or not. She propped her elbow on the desk and looked at him. ''You know, Colonel, this is the most I—we've seen of you, well, ever. Two days in a row.'' Her fingertips tapped her chin. ''It's almost enough to make a person suspicious.''

He leaned his hip against the corner of her desk, looking utterly masculine and entirely at ease. ''Because I had a meeting here this morning?'' A faint smile flirted with his mobile lips. ''I think lack of sleep is affecting your levels of paranoia, Your Royal Highness.''

Paranoia? Hardly. She only wished that seeing him twice in as many days had something to do with her personally. But she knew better.

Her gaze drifted from his long legs, over the way his uniform hugged his strong thighs and narrow hips. She was *not* prone to visualizing men without their clothes, but she realized with a mortifying flush that she was doing just that with the colonel.

And wouldn't her mother have a field day with that knowledge if she ever learned of it?

It must be a hangover from the champagne, she thought rather desperately. Champagne always had given her an aching head. And last night she'd consumed more than her share.

Meredith had no time for the frivolities of her set. She loathed the propensity for idle hands of some of the rich. She'd never gone in for the excesses of drink, the stupidity of drugs, or the mindless pursuit of as many bedmates as humanly possible.

Yet last night, she'd nearly drunk herself into oblivion. All because she'd been vilely envious of sweet Juliet Oxford's ability to get the colonel out on the dance floor.

Pierce hadn't danced with Juliet on the terrace. The thought snuck in, but Meredith resolutely ignored it. The colonel's behavior the previous evening was as much a departure from the norm as was hers.

She deliberately gathered her scattered thoughts. "You were around ten years ago," she said. "What do *you* remember about my uncle's death?"

Pierce studied Meredith's lovely face. The morning sun shining through the windows of her office ought to have illuminated any imperfections.

There were none. Only the clear deep green of her eyes as she watched him. There was nothing casual in her gaze, though her relaxed position behind her desk would have said there should be. He wasn't sure if he preferred that close look of hers or the other look. The one where she sort of focused somewhere around his ear or his chin. Looking at him without really looking at him.

If she looked too close, he was afraid she'd see straight through him.

Pierce was a strong man. With strong values, strong beliefs. But he wasn't sure he was strong enough for Meredith to see the truth inside him. At least when he held her at bay, he could be assured that she'd never know the worst. Never know him for exactly what he was.

"Colonel?"

The last time she'd used his given name, she'd been seventeen. Eleven years of wanting to see her soft lips form his name. Eleven years of wanting to hear it.

God. If this was what he got like after a sleepless night, maybe he *was* getting old.

He straightened from the desk. "There was an incident on Majorco. Edwin got caught in the crossfire."

"The wrong place at the wrong time."

"Basically."

She rubbed her fingertip against the bridge of her nose. "And the perpetrators? The people who killed my uncle. They were never found."

Pierce looked out the window, staring at the thick trees surrounding the building without really seeing them. The Royal Intelligence Institute was a jewel in the crown of Penwyck. It was world-renowned for its leading-edge research in fields from medicine to economics to music.

All of which had nothing to do with Meredith's comment.

"No." He turned to face her. "Edwin's killer was never found."

Chapter Six

Meredith sat back in her chair, folding her hands. *He has that look again,* she thought. *What is it that bothers you about my uncle?* She wanted to ask him. Would have asked him, if they'd had some semblance of comfort between them.

Instead, she dropped her hand on the computer printout for the children's center event. "It looks as if we'll be bursting at the seams at the opening of Horizons next weekend." She flipped the printout around so he could see the lengthy list. "Would you like to see it?"

He picked it up, glancing over it. "Valdosta's name is on here."

"He's a benefactor of the hospital, and the hospital is partnering with us to establish the center. Of course he'll be there."

"He'll be there because you're there," Pierce said flatly, and slid the report to her over the slick surface of the desk. "Watch out for him."

"George?" Meredith's eyebrows shot up. "Please. He's thoroughly harmless."

"Yes, if he isn't liquored like he was last night. Or perhaps I should say this morning. What would you have done if I hadn't come by when I did?"

"Kicked him in the shin as I was considering doing when you appeared. I haven't reached the age of twenty-eight without learning how to take care of myself, Colonel."

"Yes, Your Royal Highness," he said blandly. "I could see that last night."

Irritation tickled at her spine. "Last night, I was *darling*."

"Excuse me?"

She had a headache. A mountain of work awaited her attention. The smart thing would be to end the conversation immediately and get to her duties. So why was she rising? Circling her desk and going to stand by him?

"Darling," she said softly. "You called me darling last night when you got rid of George. As if you were staking your claim."

"Purely for George's benefit."

She knew it. And it pained her immensely. "Do you have any sort of personal life, Pierce?"

She'd surprised him. More by using his given name than the intrusive question, she suspected.

"Enough."

"Enough of a personal life, or enough with my questions?"

"Either."

She folded her arms, studying him. "Did it bother you? That I called you Pierce just now?"

"Of course not."

She was almost enjoying this. The unflappable colonel was generally a stickler for protocol. He had been ten years ago, and he'd been growing more so ever since. "Well, then?"

"What do you want to know, Your Royal Highness?" His expression was shuttered, belying his easy tone. "My life is an open book for you."

"Hardly." Amazed at her audacity, she reached over and smoothed her finger along the surface of the bars pinned on his shirt. "Actually, I know very little about you."

"Would you like to review my vitae? I'll have my secretary fax you one."

On anyone else, she would have taken the response for sarcasm. But with Pierce it was simply too difficult to tell.

"Personally," she clarified. She went around her desk to her briefcase and plucked out the newspaper Lillian had handed her. She flipped it open and tapped the photo that had captured them together on the terrace. "It says right there in the paper, Colonel. *Elusive.*"

He barely glanced at the photo, making his disinterest clear. "Elusive implies there is something to elude."

"Or someone."

His lips twisted slightly. "Would it make you happier if I were to tell you that there is a woman I'm eluding? Or who is eluding me?"

She slowly folded the paper and set it on her desk. "I don't know what would make me happy," she said. The honesty was more than a little painful. "Is there someone?" The words came without volition, and she wished she could draw them back.

His eyes were more silver than green today, she thought fancifully as his gaze seemed to pin her in place. There was no possible way he would answer such a question from her. It was beyond rude.

"Yes, there is someone." His lips twisted a little. "Though neither one of us is particularly successful at eluding the other, lately."

It felt like a blow to her midsection. Though there was no logical reason for his words to hurt. He was a successful, powerful, extremely charismatic man. He probably had a litter of women of whom she knew nothing. Yet he'd said *someone*. "Who is she?"

His thick, spiky lashes were very dark around his striking eyes. "I don't believe this is an—" his jaw cocked a little "—appropriate conversation, Your Royal Highness."

"Ah, yes." She forced a smile. "The age-old necessity of always being *appropriate*. Dressing appropriately. Behaving appropriately. Never, ever forgetting the most appropriate deportment under any and all circumstances." She was staring at his mouth again. Now *that* was hardly appropriate.

"Your behavior has never been less than exemplary."

"Coming from nearly anyone else, that would sound like fawning." She was accustomed to dealing with men of power. And there was no question the colonel was very much a man of power. Yet he always maintained that edge of respect for her position. And, interestingly, managed to do so without relinquishing one iota of his sense of self. His own confidence. His position. He was neither overbearing nor subservient. And he fascinated her as much as ever.

More than ever.

"And," she added wryly, "it is not entirely accurate." She tapped the newspaper.

"It's just a photo. Doesn't have to mean a thing."

"Megan and Jean-Paul thought all the speculation splashed about them in the papers meant nothing, as well. Until everyone in the land seemed to consider their relationship their business. You'll have to assure your lady friend that these photos really *were* nothing." Meredith was proud of her breezy tone. Though, frankly, she wanted to retch.

It appalled her that she could be jealous of a faceless woman, someone who'd been allowed entry into Pierce's personal life. She was too sensible, too intelligent to indulge in jealousy. Wasn't she?

"Were they nothing?"

"You just said so yourself."

He looked amused, suddenly. "I believe what I said was that the photos didn't have to mean anything."

"What's the difference?"

"I don't know, Your Royal Highness. You kissed me."

Her cheeks went hot. "And you kissed me back," she said crisply. "Explain *that* to your Ms. Elusive."

"Are you certain?"

She blinked. "About what? That you kissed me back? I know when a man has kissed me, Colonel

Prescott.'' But she *wasn't* sure. Not at all. For all she knew, she might have imagined that returned pressure of his lips. That sense that he was kissing her back, feeling some semblance of the madness that had stricken her. Imagination? Wishful thinking? It was entirely possible, whether she liked admitting it or not. Maybe it was even imagination that made it seem as if he were standing closer to her, broader and taller than ever.

His head lowered an inch, and she barely kept herself from taking an unthinkable step away from him. ''When I do kiss you, Your Royal Highness, I assure you that you'll know it.''

She locked her knees to keep them from wobbling. *''When?''*

''If.''

''It's not like you to retreat, Colonel. Or misspeak.''

He was looking just the slightest tinge harried. It made her feel immeasurably better. ''Your Royal Highness, it—''

''Why do you do that?''

''Do what?'' His tone was that of a man seeking patience.

''Your Royal Highness, *Pierce.* You always stand on ceremony. But you are a noble, after all. The Duke of Aronleigh is no small title.''

''Your point?''

''Meredith. Can't you bring yourself to say it?'' There was more pleading than challenge in the question, and Meredith wanted to cringe. ''Forget my position, for once. Is that so difficult?''

His gaze was shuttered. ''*Meredith,* you are the

daughter of my King. You will always be the daughter of my King. And that is the end of it.''

She'd forced him into addressing her by name, and there was absolutely no pleasure in it whatsoever. She didn't even know what had been spurring her on. After all, he'd admitted there was a Ms. Elusive. She was not one to step on someone else's toes when it came to relationships.

Not that she had all that much experience when it came to relationships. Despite what she'd said to Pierce about being able to take care of herself—which she *did* believe—she'd never once lost her heart to any man.

Because no man was Colonel Pierceson Prescott, the Duke of Aronleigh.

She forced herself to remain relaxed, leaning against her desk. ''Well, as pleasurable as this is—'' her voice was dry as dust ''—I do have work to do.''

''Feeling anxious?''

''Pressed for time.''

He smiled slightly. Then drew his thumb down her cheek—confusing her even more than she already was—before striding to the door. ''When you see your father, tell him I'm sorry he missed our meeting this morning.''

''He was having breakfast with my mother,'' she said faintly. Her cheek still felt the tingling heat from that barely there caress.

''With your mother.''

Behind her back, she pressed her palms against the edge of her desk. Hard. ''It's not unheard of, Colonel Prescott. We are a family, after all. One that shares meals on occasion.'' Though she had to admit it wasn't often that the King was in the residence at that hour. He was usually in his office by then.

"Of course." His expression was once again frustratingly inscrutable. "Good morning, then, Your Royal Highness."

Meredith watched him leave. When she could no longer hear his footfalls in the corridor outside her office, she sank into the nearest chair, letting out a long, shuddering breath.

When he kissed her?

If only.

Pierce could hear the laughter and high-pitched squeals of children at play all the way from Horizons, the new child-care center, to his office. He was used to working with any number of distractions, but he wasn't used to working while knowing that Meredith Penwyck was just out the door, across the tarmac, in the playground area surrounding the building the base had dedicated to the center.

Though he hadn't gone to the opening festivity and had not laid eyes on her, Pierce still knew that Meredith was there. She and Anastasia had been up to their pretty aristocratic noses in the planning for Horizons. It was his base, he'd approved the final site selection and other staffing matters for the base's contribution to the joint project, and he'd seen Meredith's and Anastasia's names on numerous memos, numerous agendas. But he had staff to handle those details, and he'd never personally involved himself in the matter beyond barely glancing at and approving the final decisions.

He trusted the decisions of his staff, for one thing.

And he trusted the judgments of Penwyck Memorial Hospital and Anastasia's contribution there for their part. As for the RII and Meredith's involvement, Pierce knew nobody could do a better job than she could. He knew that keeping his distance from her was always the wisest course.

Until lately.

Stifling an oath, he pushed aside the reports he was well over a day behind on attending to. As the files slid to one side of his metal desk, they knocked something off the edge.

He leaned over and slowly picked it up.

A microfilm cartridge.

He still couldn't believe he'd stooped to palming the small cartridge and taking it from Meredith's office when he'd been there last week. He half expected to have her hounding his heels demanding to know what was wrong with him for taking something so innocuous as microfilmed copies of decade-old newspapers. It was information she could get from any number of sources. It just might take her a little more time to accomplish.

But she hadn't even noticed. Not while he was there, at least.

His fingers tightened around the cartridge, squeezing it hard enough to crack the brittle black plastic. The sound felt like another nail being driven into his soul.

From across the way, he heard a cheer go up, and whether punishing himself or easing his grim thoughts, he stood and went to the window.

Balloons bobbed in the afternoon sunlight, tugging and jerking at the strings that attached them to nearly every immovable object. Little colored flags stretched from the building to the corner posts of the fence surrounding the play yard. And in that yard were crowds of children racing around parents, volunteers and staff. There were games, music and food.

Meredith was down there somewhere. Though he couldn't see her from his vantage point.

"Why don't you go on down there instead of standing at the window drooling like a kid outside a candy store?"

At the first word, he'd turned on his heel. "Estabon. What are you doing here? What's happened?"

The other man lifted a long hand in a calming motion. "Nothing's happened. I was accompanying the King to a meeting with the shipbuilders' federation on the North Shore."

The North Shore was less than an hour over the Aronleigh Mountains from the base's location in the north central portion of the country. It was across the island from Marlestone, a solid hundred miles.

And the King had no business conducting meetings with anyone over anything that wasn't strictly approved by the RET. He left the window and went to his office door, pushing it closed. "And you left him there?"

Sir Selwyn Estabon was the King's royal secretary. He was also a highly placed member of royal intelligence and one of Pierce's associates with the RET, a fact that was known to only the other members of the RET. And the King. The true King.

"Relax." Selwyn sat in one of the chairs facing Pierce's desk and absently brushed a speck of lint from his immaculate trousers. "Logan is with him.

When the King dismissed my services for the afternoon, I couldn't very well hang around, now could I? His security detail is with him, naturally. I'll rejoin them in a few hours.''

Duke Carson Logan served as the King's personal bodyguard. These days, Pierce likened Logan to Broderick's personal guard dog. Since Logan was the fourth member of the RET, he realized he needn't worry that Broderick would get up to too much mischief. ''Any new word on our patient?''

Selwyn shook his head, looking grim. ''This was supposed to be a one-shot deal with Broderick.'' To make one critical appearance as King Morgan to keep the alliance negotiations with Majorco moving forward. ''There was no way we could have known things would go on this long.''

''It's the King's wish,'' Pierce said flatly. The RET all knew how badly Morgan wanted the alliances to go through. Once he was on his feet, he'd have their heads if they'd let the negotiations fall through during his illness. ''I still think it was wrong not to inform Her Majesty. The law is clear. Power falls to her in the case of the King's incapacitation.''

''The King of Majorco loathes women. He wouldn't have dealt with the Queen, and the alliance would have gone dead in the water. Everything that His Majesty has worked for these past few years would have been for nothing. We all agreed with Monteque's decision to pull in the prince. Broderick may not care about Penwyck as a rule, but his ego won't let him be anything less than a great King, even if he has to be using his brother's name to do it.''

Pierce eyed Selwyn. "I think we're underestimating the Queen's abilities."

Selwyn's eyes remained steady. "I've never once underestimated her," he said smoothly. "We did what we had to do. It can't be undone now."

Pierce knew the other man was right, whether he liked it or not. "So you left him in safe hands. And you came down here because...why? To kill some time? You could have stayed on the North Shore for that. There's that one bar...what's it called? Belinda's. You remember Belinda, don't you? An American. Six feet of well-put-together blonde. Has always had a bad case for you."

Selwyn smiled ever so faintly. "Nice try. The Queen mentioned something to me the other day," he said. "I thought I'd look into it."

Selwyn was devoted to the royal family, the Queen and her daughters in particular. Pierce knew Selwyn would never consider any kind of romantic involvement with one of the Penwyck ladies. He was far too easily entertained by much less complicated relationships.

He and Selwyn were the same age, but there the similarities ended. Selwyn was honorable down to the core of his elegant being when it came to the royal women.

Pierce's gaze drifted over the cracked cartridge he'd left on his desk. He wasn't the least bit honorable. And the notion of romantic involvement with one of the Penwyck ladies was constantly plaguing him. He didn't know what was worse—thinking about Meredith during every waking hour or having her sneak into his excruciatingly vivid dreams.

None of which he intended to discuss with Selwyn, even though they were friends. "Look into what?"

"Her Majesty mentioned some concern over your interest in the princess."

"Which one? There are three."

Selwyn cocked a dark eyebrow. "Really. Yet there's only one in whom you've been taking a special interest. Enough of an interest that it's been noticed by others."

"The Queen has no need to worry about my intentions toward Meredith." If he kept telling himself that often enough, maybe he could make it true.

"Perhaps you might tell Her Majesty that yourself."

Pierce paced the confines of his austere office. "And when would I do that, Estabon? When I just happen to be dropping by the palace to check on the man posing as her husband? Or when I'm wondering whether or not to be concerned that Meredith's got it into her head to research her uncle's death?"

Selwyn sighed faintly. "There's nothing she could learn that would harm anyone."

"Except the Queen, if she knew."

"She'll never know, because we are all protecting her. Besides, you always did have an overabundance of conscience, my friend. Perhaps it's because your father was a clergyman. All that religion, you know."

"Conscience?" Pierce smiled grimly. "You couldn't be more wrong." He heard the childish cheering coming from Horizons, muffled though it was by the window, and it seemed like each joyful little shriek was an announcement of his sins. "My conscience died ten years ago when I had to face the

Queen across her brother's casket and express my condolences.''

''You did what you had to do, Pierce. And thank God for it.''

''And I'd do it again,'' he said flatly. ''Which hardly makes me the kind of man Her Majesty would like sitting at her dining room table with the family, much less courting her eldest daughter.''

''Is that what you want to do? Court Meredith? You always did have a soft spot for her.''

''It doesn't matter what I've always had,'' Pierce said flatly. ''She is a royal.''

''You have your own title, too. A duchy under your authority.''

''Earned because of killing a man.''

''Awarded for saving several others,'' Selwyn corrected evenly.

Pierce paced to the window, staring at the gleeful celebration below. He caught a glimpse of a curvaceous, leggy woman, her distinctive brunette waves pulled into a ponytail. He pressed his hand against the glass, as if he could reach out and touch her. But the distance between him and Her Royal Highness, Meredith Elizabeth of Penwyck, had never seemed greater.

''Earned. Awarded.'' He deliberately turned away from the view and tossed the microfilm cartridge into the metal trash bin beside his desk. He should have gotten rid of it the day he'd stolen it, rather than keeping it in sight to torment himself. It clattered raucously. ''What's the difference?''

Chapter Seven

"My, my, my." Anastasia leaned toward Meredith. "Look who decided to make an appearance."

Meredith grinned at the toddler on Anastasia's hip and handed the little girl an ice cream cone. She followed Anastasia's gaze, and her nerveless fingers dropped the metal scoop into the enormous cardboard container of vanilla. "He said he wasn't going to be here."

"Well—" Anastasia deliberately handed Meredith the scoop she'd dropped "—something obviously changed his mind. Or someone."

"Don't look at me."

Her sister smiled impishly. "I don't need to. The colonel is looking at you enough for us all." She whirled away with the little girl, only to be immediately surrounded by a gaggle of chattering children.

Meredith stuck the scoop into the ice cream and managed to make another somewhat rounded scoop, which she plopped into a cone and handed to the next child waiting in line. Her wrists were already aching, and she'd barely begun. She knew she could pass the task on to someone else, but there was little point to that. All the adults who were helping to run the opening celebration had tasks of their own, and it was hardly anyone's fault that the ice cream was so solidly frozen.

What she also was not going to do was stare at the colonel. It was immaterial that she hadn't been able to get him out of her thoughts since last week when he'd been in her office. When he'd spoken her name through no desire of his own. When he'd said, "*When I kiss you.*"

She winked at the little boy who was licking his lips on the other side of the table. "Chocolate or vanilla?"

"Chocolate," he said fervently, and she laughed.

"It's my favorite, too," she told him softly, and began chipping away at the ice cream. Considering it was an August afternoon, she would have thought the stuff would have begun thawing.

"Looks like you could use a hand."

Her tender palm slipped on the cold metal scoop, and her knuckles bashed into the edge of the carton. "Colonel Prescott."

He held up his hands, palms outward. "Washed and ready to serve."

At least he could put muscle behind the scoop, she thought dazedly, and handed it to him. "You said you weren't coming." She picked up a cone and held it for him to put the perfectly rounded scoop of ice cream on top. Then she handed it to the boy, who grinned and ran off.

"Vanilla," the next child whispered.

"I changed my mind." Pierce had the scoop of ice cream ready before Meredith had pulled the next cone from the sleeve. She grabbed two and held them up for him.

"Why?"

"Look at your hands."

She handed over the filled cones and grabbed two more. "What's wrong with them? Aren't I allowed to get my hands sticky in chocolate and vanilla ice cream?"

"You're allowed anything your heart desires," he said smoothly, and filled the cones. Before Meredith could reach over and hand them to the children, he plucked them from her fingers and did it himself.

One of the kids—a little girl—dropped her cone flat on her shoe. And Meredith watched in amazement as the colonel prepared another and gave the girl a little wink, making her wobbling lip turn into a wide smile and a giggle. Particularly when he topped her serving with a second round ball of ice cream.

"Now—" he pointed with the metal scoop at the rest of the children waiting in line "—that does *not* mean you can all start dumping your single scoop on the grass to get a second. Clear?"

They all nodded, eyes wide.

"So," he said to the next boy. "You want a triple or a quadruple? I'm warning you, if you want only a single, you're going to have to bribe me pretty heavily." The boy—Meredith gauged him at about ten or eleven—laughed, and Meredith's heart melted much more thoroughly than the ice cream was ever going to have a chance to do, considering how rapidly Pierce dipped it up.

"We're going to run out of ice cream at that rate," Meredith observed after a moment.

"We'll get more from the mess."

She figured he was smart enough to make his own decisions about that. So she handed him several sleeves of ice-cream cones and picked up the second metal scoop.

"No," he said abruptly.

She blinked. "Excuse me?"

"Look at your hands," he said again. And when she eyed him, he took one of her hands, flipping the palm upward. "You're getting blisters."

She curled her fingers defensively over her stinging palms and tugged away from his grasp. Aware of those in line still waiting for their treat, she smiled cheerfully. "I've never scooped up ice cream before," she said under her breath.

"And you needn't do it again."

She picked up two more cones, being careful not to crush them in her frustration. "How is it that you make me feel like a spoiled brat with very little effort at all?"

"A spoiled brat wouldn't bother with anything that took her remotely close to blisters."

She didn't take the statement as a compliment. He was far too matter-of-fact for that.

She looked at him from the corner of her eyes. Despite her personal vow not to, it was hard not to stare at Pierce. For one thing, he was out of uniform.

Wearing a short-sleeved gray shirt that hugged his broad shoulders and made his eyes look more gray than green, and a pair of blue jeans that simply went to prove why the things had been popular for more than a century.

He looked thoroughly male, and she'd have to be in a coma not to appreciate the sight of him.

"How much longer is this little soiree supposed to last?"

"Until five." She turned to the side table and opened another sleeve of cones. They were going through them at an astonishing rate. "You needn't stay if you have other things to do. I'm sure the ice cream is softening by now. I'll be able to finish up here."

"Want to get rid of me?"

She smiled wistfully. *Hardly.* "And lose a pro ice cream dipper upper like you? Of course not."

He smiled faintly. "Smart girl. Now, hand me another cone."

She felt her cheeks flush, but managed to hold out cones as he needed them, and through some miracle managed not to drop a single one.

The line was nearly finished when Pierce spoke again. "George Valdosta make it?"

"He was here earlier, but he left."

"One hundred screaming kids not his cup of tea?"

She watched him from the corner of her eyes. George Valdosta's brief visit had been the last thing on her mind. And his obvious discomfort being around all the children could be something as simple as being unaccustomed to children. Whereas the colonel seemed perfectly comfortable among the under-thirteen set.

It wasn't necessarily a trait she would have expected of him.

Commanding his troops, keeping his thumb on the pulse of national and international intelligence, even piloting a plane or rolling around in the muck. But dipping up ice-cream cones for a hoard of excited children?

It was a side of the colonel that sent an unfamiliar tug through her.

A tug that continued throughout the afternoon. As Meredith had predicted, they did run out of ice cream, and as promised, Pierce called for more from the base's kitchen. And after all the children had eaten their cones, and second and sometimes a third one, he pitched in with finger painting. Then face painting. Egg tosses and sack races.

If he weren't in the thick of things, Meredith had only to look a few feet and she'd find him tying a child's shoelace, wiping a nose or pulling a coin from behind the ear of a wide-eyed little one.

She never expected he'd stick it out until five o'clock. Not only did he do so, personally seeing off every family that had attended the opening celebration, but he remained afterward. Moving tables and chairs inside the center. Washing up sticky floors and carrying out mammoth bags of trash.

Anastasia, on her way out because of another engagement that evening, stopped beside Meredith and nudged her arm meaningfully. "Did you see the way he wiped down the wall those kids had taken a marker to? Not a spot left."

Meredith flexed her back. She was exhausted and had a new appreciation for anyone who provided care for more than one child at a time. "So?"

"So?" Anastasia leaned closer, her eyes glinting with mischief. "*That* is a man who knows how to attend to details."

"Anastasia!"

Her sister lifted innocent shoulders then brushed a kiss over Meredith's cheeks. "I'm sorry I have to cut out before all the dirty work is finished."

Meredith laughed. "Yes, sweetie, I can tell by the smile on your face just how very sorry you are."

"I'd rather stay here than have to make an appearance at the hospital benefit tonight."

"Absolutely." Meredith nodded seriously. "Scrubbing donated toys and picking up pieces of popped balloons so nobody decides to eat them is far preferable to dining under the stars."

Anastasia's gaze drifted past Meredith's shoulder. "Depends on the company, I'd say." She smiled again, and with a wave to everyone still working around the center, hurried away to the silver limousine that was waiting for her.

Meredith hadn't needed Anastasia's glance to know who'd come up behind her. She'd sensed Pierce all on her own.

"Anastasia taking off?"

Schooling her features, Meredith dropped the sponge she'd been using to wash a tabletop into the bucket beside her and glanced at Pierce. "Yes. There's a benefit on her schedule for this evening."

"And you?"

She was generally considered to be a highly intelligent person. Yet with Pierce, she felt as if the only thing guiding her were rudimentary instincts. "And I what?"

"What are you doing this evening?" he elaborated patiently.

She leaned back against the table. "With luck, having a foot massage." She wriggled her feet. Her tennis shoes had been pristine white that morning, but were now spotted with ice-cream drips and grass stains. The rest of her hadn't fared much better. "Though a shower first is probably in order. I look a mess."

"You should have had other people handling the messy stuff."

"Why? I can't get blisters on my palms or stains on my shirt like other people?"

Pierce took her hand, startling her into silence, and turned it over. He tsked at her hastily curled fingers, and with little effort spread them flat. "You need bandages on them."

"My palms are a little raw." Her voice was blithe. "But not blistered."

He curtailed the impulse to lift her palms to his lips. "They shouldn't even be raw."

"Why not? Because I'm Meredith, Princess of Penwyck? You take your duty to protect the King and his family far too seriously, I think. There *is* a woman under my title."

A woman he wanted under him. Over him. All around him. A thought that was beyond inappropriate. He released her hand and picked up the bucket. "I'll have someone from the infirmary come over to tend your hands."

Meredith wanted to tear out her hair by the roots. "Colonel," she said crisply, "I do not need anyone to tend to my poor little hands. The country's health-care system is not going to crash to a halt because I have some tender red marks on my palms from wres-tling with an ice-cream scoop and a mop!"

His lips twitched. "Feel a little strongly about that, do you, Meredith?"

Her heart seemed to stop beating. Meredith. He'd called her Meredith. With no maneuvering whatso-ever on her part.

She swallowed past the lump that suddenly lodged in her throat. "Yes, as a matter of fact, I do," she said honestly. "I receive enough special treatment as it is. I certainly don't need to pull people away from their duties."

"All right, then *you* go to the infirmary and get your hands taken care of."

She wanted to grin like a silly fool. The man had a singular ability for sending her emotions all over the spectrum with no more than a blink of his eye. "How about if I just get some adhesive bandages from the first-aid kit inside that cupboard over there."

Pierce smiled faintly. Meredith in a saucy mode was something to behold. "Might work."

She turned with a flip of her ponytail and strode to the cupboard in question. She might have said she was a mess, but in truth, Pierce thought she looked better than ever. It was a common sight to see Mer-edith in designer gowns and the couturier suits she favored. But to see her in trim red shorts that made her long legs go on forever with a strappy little yellow tank top that clung to her womanly curves was a pure pleasure.

Almost as much a pleasure as hearing her laughter ringing out all afternoon, as seeing her pitch in with her entire being at tasks with which she'd obviously had little experience. It had nearly made him lose his head, in fact. Coming close to asking her to spend the evening with him was about as dangerous a notion as he could have envisioned, yet he'd been on the verge of doing just that.

Fortunately, she hadn't picked up on it.

She came back and presented her palms, decorated with printed bandages.

He chuckled at the sheer delight in her expression. "That's all it takes to make you happy? Cartoon-printed bandages?"

"Actually, it's the fluorescent pink and blue ones that I'm particularly fond of." She looked at her palms, wiggling her long, slender fingers. "I tried one of each pattern from the container." A fact that made her positively glow, as if she'd slid diamond rings on each finger instead of garish bandages across nearly every inch of her palms.

"Good thing we locked out the media from this particular event," he said dryly. "They'd get photos of your hands and start speculating that the royal coffers were bankrupt, sending the eldest royal daughter to buckets and mops."

"Completely ignoring any marketability I might have in the professional world with my advanced degrees in economics and political science."

"The mop bucket would make for a more salacious story."

She straightened a few more child-size chairs and waved to the last few volunteers as they took their leave. "Not every story in the media is angled for that. Some *do* report the truth."

And some report what they're told is the truth, he thought, wishing he'd never broached the subject. He deliberately looked around. "It looks to me like all the work here's done."

She nodded, also looking around at the cheerful interior of Horizons. Bright white walls were made vivid with hand-painted murals depicting everything from cartoon characters to fairy-tale scenes. There was an area for naps, an area for play, for eating and for studying. Her shoulders lifted and fell in a faint sigh.

"What's wrong?"

She brushed back a loose strand of hair. "It took us two years to get this place off the ground. Between the hospital and the RII and then the red tape of your base—" she eyed him "—and now it is all set for business, starting Monday, and..." She shrugged. "And my part in it is over."

"Only if you want it to be. There is still an oversight committee."

"On which people far more qualified than I am are already sitting." She picked up a stuffed bear that someone had left sitting on one of the counters and tugged at the ears for a moment before taking it over to the toy chests and setting it on top of the overflowing mound.

"Why was this project so important to you, anyway?"

She looked at him, her clear green eyes surprised. "Because the children around here need it."

The facility wasn't open only to children of the base, but the families in the surrounding communities, as well, right up into the Aronleigh Mountains. And while the base did have a small child-care center, they'd had continual difficulty keeping it staffed based on their budget constraints. The plan Meredith had come up with, dragging in the RII and Penwyck Memorial Hospital, would effectively overcome what the base hadn't accomplished on its own. It was a good plan. And he'd been proud of her abilities in bringing it to fruition.

He watched her pick up another toy, then twitch a corner of a window curtain into place. "You ought to be having kids of your own."

After one brief look, her lashes swept down and she strode to the utility cupboard and pulled open the door. "Considering that my mother, at my age, had already had three children, you mean?"

"I don't mean anything except that the kids adored you today. You'd be great with some of your own."

"One could say the same thing about you, Colonel. You were very good with the children today." She stuck the mop in the closet and waited for him to put the emptied bucket on the shelf.

"You sound surprised."

"Well, I guess I am." She closed the closet door and locked it with the key that hung on a high peg on the wall. "Maybe. A little."

"A nicely definitive answer." He caught her faint smile. "I'm thirty-five and set in my ways."

Her eyebrows shot up. "Oh, please. You make thirty-five sound ancient."

"Feels that way sometimes."

She shook her head, muttering something under her breath as she went around slapping off the light switches until she came to the doorway.

"If you have something to say, Your Royal Highness, then just say it. There's no point to beating around the bush."

She turned to face him, the lowering evening sun lighting her from behind. "Back to 'Your Royal Highness' again," she said, sounding annoyed. "All right. I said that thirty-five on you looks rather phenomenal to me." Her hands lifted then fell to her sides. "But then you know what I think about you. You've always known. Whether we've ever had a civilized discussion, devoid of bush beating, about it or not. And please do me the courtesy of keeping your false denials to yourself."

"It really does annoy you that I don't forget your heritage. You bring it up often enough."

She stepped out the door, and the sunset outlined the perfection of her profile. "Nowhere near as often as you put it squarely between us. So, yes. It really annoys me. If you have no interest in me, have never had any interest in me and all these years I've been imagining the—the *whatever* it is between us, then just say so. I'll adjust. But if not—" she closed her eyes for a moment, then lifted her chin in that regal way that always drove him more than a little nuts "—if not, then I really wish for once that you would look at me and simply see the woman. Not the princess."

Pierce slowly walked over to her. She flipped the lock on the doorknob and pulled it shut behind them. He should never have let Selwyn Estabon goad him into joining the festivity. His instincts to stay away had been right on the money. Because every minute he spent in Meredith's company he felt himself sinking ever deeper into emotions he'd denied for too damn long.

"What I wish, Meredith, is that I could look at you just once and *not* see the woman, but only the princess."

Her soft lips parted, and her eyes suddenly filled with a liquid sheen that made the ache deep inside him intensify tenfold. "I—"

"But it doesn't matter." He forced the words. "Nothing can come of it."

"Because of your Ms. Elusive?"

He cupped her jaw, watching her eyes flicker. "You don't get it. *You* are the elusive one. Only you."

"Pierce—"

He smoothed his thumb gently over her lips. "Don't."

She caught his wrist in both her hands. But she didn't pull it away. And she closed her eyes, pressing a kiss against this thumb, nearly undoing any good intentions he tried to maintain. "Please," she whispered.

She could be his salvation. Or his undoing. Either was too dangerous to contemplate.

"I'll end up hurting you," he muttered. His fingers slid from the silky arch of her jaw to her nape. Molding the shape of her head.

"You don't know that."

"I do know."

She let go of his wrist and slid her hands up his chest. Touching his neck, his jaw. "Pierce—"

"Meredith, we can't." He pressed his lips against her temple. "I can't."

"Won't."

"The results are the same."

She made a soft sound. "It was easier when we rarely saw each other, and then only during some meeting or other."

"Yes."

She pulled back her head, searching his face. "I don't understand you at all."

"Don't waste the effort trying. Go out with George Valdosta if he can stay sober enough to behave. Better yet, find someone who *is* good enough for you. Live your life. Fall in love. Get married. Have kids."

"I'd like to," she said huskily. "Except I think we both know you're the only man I've ever been able to think of in those kind of terms. So you might as well just kiss me now, Pierce. Because the hurting began long ago."

"Dammit, Meredith—"

"One kiss," she whispered, stepping closer. "Just one kiss—"

He'd always been a sinner. When he covered her mouth with his, though, it felt like he'd been granted a glimpse of heaven.

Chapter Eight

He tasted of chocolate, and the coffee she'd noticed someone bringing him partway through the afternoon. He tasted of Pierce. He tasted right. Just exactly right.

And when he pulled away, sucking in a harsh breath, she was dimly aware that the moaning little sound of dismay had come from her. He tucked her head in the curve between his shoulder and neck that seemed as though it had been designed strictly with her in mind, and she felt his heart beating hard through the soft fabric of his shirt.

It matched hers beat for racing beat.

"I knew this was a bad idea," he muttered, his lips burning along her temple.

"No." She twisted, trying to find his lips, and when he evaded her, she pressed her mouth against his neck. Tasted the pulse throbbing at the base. "It's good,'' she murmured against him. ''Very, very good.''

Her lips nibbled the sharp blade of his jaw, the small dent in his chin. Whispered over his lips, sighed his name when, with a husky oath, he covered her mouth with his, surrounding her with his arms, pulling her tight against him.

Her senses simply exploded.

Then it was only racing hands and marauding kisses. Kisses that had been years in the waiting, and were, impossibly, all the more sweet for it. His hair felt like silk between her fingers, and his scent filled her head. She could no more fight the rampant emotion flooding her veins than she could resist touching him. Holding him. Wanting him in ways that went far beyond physical.

''Bloody hell.'' His voice was rough, barely audible, barely cutting through her senses.

But then he yanked her hands away from his neck, and Meredith gasped, swayed, as he backed away from where he'd pressed her against the door. She breathed his name, instinctively reached for him.

He moved away. ''We can't do this.''

Her lips were still tingling, her breath tumbling past her swollen lips. ''I thought we were doing quite well.'' Her voice was faint.

He raked back his hair. ''We're nearly standing out in the middle of my *base*.''

She couldn't believe her daring and blamed it on the dazed cloud fogging her brain. ''We could go some—''

''No!''

He began pacing back and forth in front her. Five

short strides one way. Five the other. Looking like some caged animal, desperate for freedom. "We do that, and you're going to end up in my bed."

"You don't want me in your bed?"

He bared his teeth a little. "Meredith, I swear, you'd try the patience of Job."

The cloud around her was clearing rapidly enough to cause her a physical ache. She tugged down the hem of her shirt. "My mother used to tell me that when I was five and begging to accompany her on her foreign engagements."

"I'd say my reaction to you and your mother's re-action to you are somewhat different." His tone was arid.

Meredith pushed her fingertips inside her front pockets to keep from fidgeting. "Undoubtedly."

"What am I going to do with you?"

"If you're asking for suggestions, I'd be happy to remind you that—"

He lifted a hand. "Enough."

She tucked the tip of her tongue between her teeth for a moment. "I'm sorry," she said, striving for some humor, when all she felt like doing was throwing herself humiliatingly into his arms again, "but you do realize that you've just shushed a princess."

"I've just about mauled a princess," he muttered.

And he looked terrifically upset about it. "I'd hardly term it that. Rumpled her feathers some, maybe."

He looked upward, as if for patience. "Darling, we didn't rumple, we burned."

"I thought it was pretty fabulous, actually. Burning." She couldn't help it if she sounded diffident.

The man completely unnerved her. Derailed her usual composure. Set her swinging on a pendulum from delirium to desperation, and while it was absolutely too tantalizing to step away from, there *was* a small portion of her brain that wondered what kind of insanity she was entertaining.

"*Fabulous* only goes so far."

She was sickeningly aware that she understood him not one bit more than she ever had. "I'll have to take your word on that since my experience of fabulous is somewhat limited."

He didn't look as if that statement comforted him any, either. In fact, he looked…well, he looked grim and fierce, and except for the shirt that she must have tugged half loose from his belt, he looked perfectly normal. As if nothing momentous had just occurred between them.

But maybe it really had only been momentous to her, after all.

She smoothed her ponytail, annoyed to see that her hands were still trembling. Annoyed to know that while he'd been pressed against her so closely that not even a sigh could have slid between them, she hadn't been annoyed by her trembling in the least.

And she was excruciatingly annoyed that there was an ominous burning behind her eyes. Because she absolutely was *not* going to cry in front of Pierce. Tears were simply and utterly unacceptable.

Which meant she needed to leave. Immediately.

But as soon as the thought hit her, she remembered she'd driven herself to the event rather than ridden in the limousine with Anastasia, as she'd known her sister would have to leave early. She'd need her car keys for her car. Car keys that were safely tucked inside her small little purse. The small little purse she'd forgotten inside Horizons. On the other side of the door she'd already locked.

All of which made her feel even more infuriatingly close to tears.

"I need to get inside," she said stiffly. "Would you be so kind as to call one of the staffers to come and let me in? You should have a phone roster in the material we've sent you."

He eyed her closely. "There's no more work to be done inside."

"My purse and car keys are locked in there." Admitting it made her feel foolish. As if she weren't capable of managing even the most ordinary of tasks.

Like dipping up ice cream.

"You're leaving."

"Is there any reason to stay?" She knew the answer to that. Of course she did. She was an intelligent woman, after all. So why, when he merely said they'd go across to his office and he'd call someone, did she feel a last bit of hope inside her wither to nothing?

She followed him to the big building across from Horizons and up four flights to his office. He was a colonel and a nobleman. Yet his office was barely half the size of her dressing room.

The metal desk faced away from the window. No doubt he wouldn't want to be tempted with something so mundane as staring out the window and daydreaming. Behind the desk was a chair that looked as if it dated from the 1950s. Or before. A round metal trash bin sat beside the desk, and four filing cabinets filled one of the walls. In front of the desk sat two wooden straight-back chairs, precisely aligned.

Other than the mammoth stack of files and books and papers on top of the desk, it was sterile and austere and verging on dreary.

"You need a plant. A painting. Something to look at in here other than oddly yellow walls."

"So my secretary tells me." He lifted the phone and spoke into it briefly. Then he turned and leaned against the edge of the desk. "Someone will be by to undo the lock in a few minutes. I hadn't realized you'd driven yourself."

"I *do* drive."

"I know. But the mountains around here aren't quite what you're used to down around Marlestone."

"And since I can't manage to keep track of my keys without locking them away, I probably can't manage to navigate myself safely around anything but the simplest of roads? Really, Pierce. Hold onto your hat, but not only have I driven all over Penwyck from North Shore to the south, I've also driven in other countries. In America, even. On the wrong side of the road."

"I never suggested you were incapable."

She ignored him. Gave him as wide a berth as the confining office allowed, and moved to look out the window. The moment she saw someone approach Horizons, she would head down there, she silently vowed.

She stared at the window, gradually noticing the precise imprint of a hand on the glass, knowing by the size of the palm print, the length of the square-tipped fingers, that it was Pierce's. "Why did you go down there today?"

He didn't answer immediately. "Horizons *is* on my base."

"It was on your base when you declined to participate when we were arranging the day. One of your aides gave the welcome speech, even." She slowly lifted her hand and fit it within the print on the glass. "You changed your mind. Why?"

"I ended up with a free afternoon, after all."

She looked over her shoulder, eyeing the materials nearly overwhelming the surface of his desk. She knew he was closely involved in the alliances, and those particular matters weren't allowing anyone extra time these days. "Right." She returned her attention to the window. It was growing dark, and lights were flicking on around the grounds. On the corners of buildings, atop tall lampposts beside the roads, on the ground along the walkways.

"Boredom?"

The fenced-in playground across the way looked peaceful, all signs of the opening celebration gone. The swings were still. The merry-go-round's bright-blue paint glistened under the floodlight at the corner of the lot. The slide was a silent sentry, and the sandbox and the heavy-duty rubber tires that were arranged in an obstacle course looked like secrets in the dusk. It all looked perfect as it lay in wait for the next child to race from one structure to the next, laughing and playing.

"I think you stood up here this afternoon in your austere, monklike office, looked down there at the balloons and banners and children and wanted to be part of something vital and cheerful,'' she said softly.

''I didn't think any of your degrees were in psychology.''

''They weren't.''

''Then I suggest you not quit your day job.''

She slowly pulled her palm away from the window. She'd left a print, also. Perfectly aligned within his larger one. ''Then why?'' She turned to face him, but he was still leaning against his desk, looking toward the door. Not looking at her at all. ''Why did you go down there?''

''I wanted ice cream. I wanted to see if I could remember how to pull coins from someone's ear. I wanted to get some fresh air. I wanted to see up close the people who'll be a regular part of base life from here on out. Take your pick or make up your own reasoning, I don't care.''

''What *do* you care about?'' She saw his shoulders flex against the soft fabric of his shirt, and she moved until she could look into his face. That beautiful face that looked as if it had been carved in granite for all the emotion he allowed to show.

Except in his eyes. Where a wealth of shadows spoke of things, painful things, of which she knew nothing. It hurt to see those shadows. To know that he held something deep inside him that caused them. To know that she could wish upon a million stars and never be able to help him shed light on them, disperse the shadows once and for all.

''I care about Penwyck.''

Such a simple statement, yet one that encompassed so much. ''I asked my father once what he cared

about.'' She smiled faintly, tugging her ear. ''I believe I was nineteen and filled with high-minded ide-
als learned at university, and we were debating something. I can't even remember what. But I remember
asking him that. What he cared about. He said that
very same thing. 'I care about Penwyck.' ''

She wandered to the window. There was still no
sign of anyone tending to the locked door across the
way. ''In general, most citizens would say they cared
about their country. But with my father, it meant so
much more than that. He'd die for his people if he
had to. So would you.''

''Yes.''

''Honor,'' she murmured. ''It's a powerful thing.''
She looked over her shoulder when she heard the
scrape of one of the chairs against the tile floor. He'd
risen and was straightening the edge of some thick
books atop one of the file cabinets. Sighing a little,
she looked out the window. A uniformed soldier was
crouched by the door of the center. She saw it swing
inward.

''The door's unlocked.'' She moved away from the
window and headed out of his office, down the hall.
He went with her. ''You needn't see me out,'' she
said smoothly. ''I imagine I'll find my way just fine.''

''Meredith.''

''What?''

''Shut up.''

She blinked. And stood in silence as he punched
the button for the elevator. They rode down in silence,
and he waited while she went into the building to
retrieve her purse from the shelf on which she'd left
it. Then he walked her out to the VIP parking lot and

held the door for her as she sank down into her sporty little roadster.

He slowly pushed the door closed, his hands resting over the top of the door. Close enough to brush her shoulder if he wished. Close enough for her to press a kiss to his knuckles if she dared.

She swallowed and pushed the key in the ignition. Her temperamental car was serviced weekly by the palace. It started with a soft purr. "Well. Whatever your real reasons were—" she didn't dare look at him "—I'm glad that you did decide to join us. The children and parents were very happy you were there." *So was I.*

"I went because I couldn't stay away from you."

Her fingers curled tightly around the steering wheel. She blinked furiously.

"Are you crying?"

"No!" Only she made the mistake of looking at him.

His expression softened, which didn't help Meredith in the least. It was easier to hold the emotions inside her when he looked as immovable as a hunk of granite. But when his changeable eyes deepened, and the tight line of his lips relaxed, pulling eons from his age, she could feel herself dissolving.

"This is my fault," he said gruffly, and lifted his hand, looking pained when she leaned back, bumping her head against the headrest. He continued the motion, though, and slowly thumbed away the tear that was slipping down her cheek. "I knew I would hurt you."

"Damned if you do, damned if you don't," Meredith said, but the effect of the tart words was somewhat lost beneath the huskiness of her voice. "You'll hurt me if you avoid me, you'll hurt me if you don't avoid me, you'll hurt me if you l-love me." She shrugged, striving for nonchalance and failing miserably. "You might just as well have taken me to bed, Pierce. Then at least you'd have something in exchange for all this trouble."

"Making love is a hell of a lot more important than an exchange," he said.

"Right. Whatever you say."

"Meredith, don't sit there and act as if you blithely sleep around in exchange for anything. You're too—"

"Cold? Removed? Uppity? I believe all the terms have been applied to me at one point or another."

"Too honorable."

She swallowed, wondering if she'd ever be rid of the lump in her throat. "Honor doesn't keep you warm at night," she whispered. "And as it happens, the issue's never been put to the test."

"What's that supposed to mean?"

"Think about it." She deliberately put the car into gear. Glanced at him once more, because she couldn't prevent it. He was the man who'd filled her heart for so long, the man who'd eclipsed any other who might have had the slightest chance for her to feel something for, and she didn't even really know who Pierce was. She did know, however, that future contact between them would be as scarce as it had always been. Considering everything, it was probably a good thing, even if it did send a weird sort of grief throbbing through her. Her hands tightened even more on the steering wheel until her knuckles stood out, white. This really was it, then. "Goodbye, Colonel."

He slowly removed his hands from the door and stepped away from the car, a tall, stern-looking man with a military bearing and shadows in his eyes. "Goodbye, Your Royal Highness."

Chapter Nine

The crowd being held back by several police officers was the first indication Pierce had that something unusual was happening at the main library in Sterling.

The sight of the long, gleaming silver limousine, parked in front of the steps of the hundred-year-old brick building as he drove past, was the second.

It was Friday evening, and as far as Pierce knew, the library closed early and stayed closed through the weekend during the summer months. He also knew there were only a few of those distinctive silver limos on the island, and as he drove his car into his reserved parking space at his apartment building, he wondered which member of the royal family was conducting business after hours at the Sterling Library.

Broderick had been more or less under control for the past week, according to Pierce's conversations with Estabon and Logan and Monteque. Despite increasing tensions as the day drew near, everything was progressing toward the signing of the alliances, making it seem as if the RET's decision to engage in the masquerade had been the right one.

The Queen might possibly have an engagement at the library, he thought. She was a strong supporter of literacy efforts. The knot in his gut, though, warned Pierce most effectively that it could well be Meredith just down the block and past the park next to his apartment building.

He hadn't seen her since she'd driven away from the base nearly a week ago.

He hadn't needed to see her to be tormented by her, however. Visions of her in his sleeping and waking dreams were more than enough to accomplish that.

He stopped at the mailbox and retrieved a mammoth amount of mail—most of it junk—and carried it to his upstairs flat. He hadn't been there all week, and he went around the place, throwing open the windows to get rid of the closed-in smell. He had a service that came in regularly, so every surface gleamed and the refrigerator was stocked. Something he silently blessed when he pulled open the door and grabbed a tall, cold beer. It might not be all that fashionable in Penwyck, but he wanted his beer cold. Damn near icy.

He yanked loose the tie that had been strangling him throughout a day of endless meetings, all pertaining to the pending alliances, and stepped onto the narrow balcony overlooking the front of the building. Tilting the beer to his lips, he leaned over the wrought-iron railing and stared down the block at the cluster of people and the silver limousine.

He watched until his beer was down halfway. Then he went in and grabbed the telephone. In minutes, he knew that there were no official reasons for anyone to be at the Sterling Library. He also knew that his gut instinct had been right on the money. Meredith had been in Sterling because she'd had to make a quick trip across to Drogheda that afternoon.

He went to the terrace and slowly toyed with the beer bottle as he watched some more. What was Meredith doing at a closed library? He knew, even before he set down the unfinished beer, that he'd have to go over there and find out. Curiosity, wariness and a plain unvarnished need to see her again.

Sterling was the major port between Penwyck and the neighboring islands of Drogheda to the east and Majorco to the south, and the majority of the island's population lived in either Sterling or Marlestone. If Pierce had to describe the differences between the two cities, he'd say that Sterling was a bit more cosmopolitan, a bit more modern and freewheeling. Undoubtedly because the palace of the ruling family didn't overlook the city as it did in Marlestone.

In any case, though it was the dinner hour on a Friday evening, traffic was more than brisk, so he left his car and walked down the block toward the library. He'd been surprised at how much he'd come to like the flat once he'd taken it. It was far larger than one man needed on his own, of course. But it had been a good investment, and it had proven to be an escape for him when he went there just as much as it was an escape for those who lived and worked on the base to be rid of him now and again.

He neared the limousine and went around to say hello to the driver before making his way to the police officers who were holding the people at bay. Pierce was fairly well known, and he easily worked his way around the officials and headed up the steps and inside.

He paused in the marbled foyer, glancing to his left. Fiction. To his right. Non-fiction. Or upstairs. Periodicals.

Sighing, he headed for the stairs. When he saw her, sitting at the end of a long, narrow table, her head bent over a newspaper, he sighed again. Dammit. The woman was too curious by far.

He slowly walked across the floor, thinking that the library was much too quiet. Which was a ludicrous thought, all things considered. He spoke before he reached the table, as he had no particular desire to scare her out of her wits. "Checking out the job listings?"

She wasn't startled in the least, however. She slid her hand down the length of her hair, which pooled onto the table near her shoulder, and looked at him. She wore a sexy little pair of spectacles that perched on her even sexier patrician nose. "Since ice-cream-parlor work is probably not going to work well for me," she said, "I thought it wise."

God, she was lovely.

"So, you thought being driven here to Sterling in a limo bearing the royal colors, you'd be able to peruse the ads in private."

"You're so quick. I was in Drogheda, which I'm sure you know very well."

She looked at the newspaper. Folded it neatly along the creases and set it in a stack to one side before reaching for a paper from a second stack to the other side. "Funny, isn't it, that the RII, known for its research departments, only had one microfilm of newspapers issued a decade ago, and somehow I managed to lose it before getting a chance to even read it."

His nerves knotted a little. He picked up one of the papers she'd clearly finished with and unfolded it so he could see the masthead. It was, indeed, dated ten years ago. But it wasn't a newspaper from Marlestone, or Sterling, or anywhere on Penwyck, for that matter. It was from Majorco. "Planning on getting a job across the way?"

"Very funny." She flipped closed the newspaper she'd just opened. "I've already been through these papers. Twice. Do you know how often my uncle's name was mentioned? Once." She leaned over and leafed through the stack to her right. Pulled out one, and flipped it open to one of the last pages. She stabbed at a small, very brief obituary. "That's it."

"Edwin wasn't well known on Majorco. On Penwyck, the citizens were aware that he was the brother of their Queen. You know as well as I do that back then the two countries had little to do with one another."

"Yet he was killed in some sort of subversive incident while on a business trip in Majorco." She made a face and rapidly folded the paper. "Penwyck's papers said hardly anything else. And what business was he conducting on Majorco, anyway?

Mother said that Edwin dabbled in all sorts of things, but as far as I can tell, he didn't have a particular career per se.''

"Dabbling can be done anywhere. I understood he spent most of his time in London. Your mother may have transplanted to Penwyck from her London home when she married the King, but that didn't mean her brother did, as well." He salved his conscience with the fact that his words were the truth. Just not the entire truth.

A lie by omission is still a lie, Pierce could hear his father, the minister, saying from long ago.

He ignored it and concentrated on Meredith.

"I know." She'd propped her chin on her hand and was drawing off her glasses. "I *know.*''

She had dark circles beneath her eyes. "You look tired."

"How good you are for my ego."

"Meredith—"

She suddenly shoved her chair back and rose, snatching up the newspapers. "If you're going to start in about last Saturday, don't. I couldn't be less interested." She disappeared between two narrow shelves.

Pierce picked up her eyeglasses. Held them up.

"They're real enough," she said as she walked into sight, sans newspapers.

"I didn't know you wore glasses."

"You don't know many things about me."

"I know that whenever you or one of your siblings so much as changes your hairstyle or favored clothing designer, it makes all the newspapers and television reports."

"So it's my little secret," she drawled, and took

them from him. She folded them up and slid them into an invisible pocket on the side of her pale green suit jacket. Then she leaned over and picked up her briefcase, and the deep V of her jacket gaped a little, giving Pierce a killing glimpse of ivory lace and taut ivory skin. If he were the honorable man she seemed to think he was, he'd look away.

She straightened, and her jacket fell right back into its perfectly cut lines. "Well, if we count the wedding day events all as one, we've now seen each other a total of four times, including now. That ought to be enough to spread out for the next full year, don't you think? Given the frequency of our contact over the past...well, enough years that it'll make *me* sound ancient if I admit to it." She didn't look at him as she headed for the staircase.

"Have dinner with me."

She stopped walking but didn't look at him. "Excuse me?"

"You heard me."

She turned on one slender, spiky heel. "Perhaps I have commitments this evening."

"You don't."

"And how do you know?"

"I checked."

"Oh, of course." Her lips stretched into a false smile. "You are the king of intelligence, after all. You probably only needed to make one phone call and my entire public schedule was transmitted to your wristwatch or some such equally spylike device."

"You're confusing me with James Bond."

"He, at least, was a man a woman could understand."

GIFTS from the Heart

Play Gifts from the Heart and get 2 FREE Books and a FREE Gift!

HOW TO PLAY:

1. With a coin, carefully scratch off the gold area at the right. Then check the claim chart to see what we have for you — **2 FREE BOOKS** and a **FREE GIFT** — **ALL YOURS FREE!**

2. Send back the card and you'll receive two brand-new Silhouette Special Edition® novels. These books have a cover price of $4.50 each in the U.S. and $5.25 each in Canada, but they are yours to keep absolutely free.

3. There's no catch. You're under no obligation to buy anything. We charge nothing —**ZERO** — for your first shipment. And you don't have to make any minimum number of purchases — not even one!

4. The fact is, thousands of readers enjoy receiving books by mail from the Silhouette Reader Service™. They enjoy the convenience of home delivery... they like getting the best new novels at discount prices, **BEFORE** they're available in stores...and they love their *Heart to Heart* subscriber newsletter featuring author news, horoscopes, recipes, book reviews and much more!

5. We hope that after receiving your free books you'll want to remain a subscriber. But the choice is yours — to continue or cancel, any time at all! So why not take us up on our invitation, with no risk of any kind. You'll be glad you did!

A surprise gift FREE!

We can't tell you what it is... but we're sure you'll like it! A

FREE GIFT!

Visit us online at www.eHarlequin.com

just for playing **GIFTS FROM THE HEART!**

PLAY GIFTS from the Heart

Scratch off the gold area with a coin.
Then check below to see the gifts you get!

YES! I have scratched off the gold area. Please send me the 2 Free books and gift for which I qualify. I understand I am under no obligation to purchase any books as explained on the back and on the opposite page.

335 SDL DNSK   235 SDL DNSF

FIRST NAME

LAST NAME

ADDRESS

APT.#

CITY

STATE/PROV.

ZIP/POSTAL CODE

| ♥ ♥ ♥ ♥ 2 free books plus a surprise gift |
| ♥ ♥ ♥ 2 free books   ♥ ♥ 1 free book |

Offer limited to one per household and not valid to current
Silhouette Special Edition® subscribers. All orders subject to approval.

(S-SE-05/02)

The Silhouette Reader Service™ — Here's how it works:

Accepting your 2 free books and gift places you under no obligation to buy anything. You may keep the books and gift a return the shipping statement marked "cancel." If you do not cancel, about a month later we'll send you 6 additional bo and bill you just $3.80 each in the U.S., or $4.21 each in Canada, plus 25¢ shipping & handling per book and applicable taxes if any.* That's the complete price and — compared to cover prices of $4.50 each in the U.S. and $5.25 each in Canada — it's quite a bargain! You may cancel at any time, but if you choose to continue, every month we'll send you 6 more books, which you may either purchase at the discount price or return to us and cancel your subscription.

*Terms and prices subject to change without notice. Sales tax applicable in N.Y. Canadian residents will be charged applicable provincial taxes and GST.

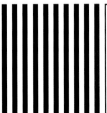

BUSINESS REPLY MAIL
FIRST-CLASS MAIL   PERMIT NO. 717-003   BUFFALO, NY

POSTAGE WILL BE PAID BY ADDRESSEE

SILHOUETTE READER SERVICE
3010 WALDEN AVE
PO BOX 1867
BUFFALO NY 14240-9952

NO POSTAGE
NECESSARY
IF MAILED
IN THE
UNITED STATES

"And you still haven't answered."

She tilted her head, considering. "You're right. I haven't." She turned and started down the steps. In moments, he heard the squeak of the heavy front door.

Well, what had he expected? That she'd forget about the way he'd pushed her away the last time they'd been together? That she'd fall into his arms like some besotted little flower?

Meredith was intelligent and very much her own woman. If the country had different laws when it came to succession to the throne, she could well have been the next ruler when King Morgan died, instead of one of her younger brothers.

Shoving his hands through his hair, Pierce headed for the steps. He definitely did not need to be thinking even remotely about the death of King Morgan. Right now, the King needed every positive thought of those close to him.

When Pierce left the library, it was to the sight of Meredith, standing among the crowd, patiently shaking hands, smiling and speaking with everyone as if she hadn't just spent the day doing similar tasks at two different functions in Drogheda on behalf of the RII.

She made no indication whatsoever that she noticed when he rounded the crowd and headed down the street, past the park and toward his building.

Once in his apartment, he headed onto the balcony and looked down the street. The crowd was dispersing, and the limousine was nowhere in sight.

Restless, he went inside. The idea of an uneventful, nonworking evening that had held some vague appeal only a few hours ago no longer appealed. At least on duty, he could bury his head in work. Here, in this spacious apartment, there seemed little to do. Except think about Meredith.

"You're getting damned sad," he muttered, and went into his bedroom, shucking his uniform as he went. He'd get dressed and go down to the pub. Or to an early show. He'd eat rare steak and drink fine wine, and drag out his phone book and look up old friends. Female friends.

Nothing like the company of a willing woman to make a man forget another.

Meredith had been more than willing until you blew it.

He balled up his shirt and pitched it into the hamper, annoyed with himself, with his thoughts, with the fact that no matter how dangerous he knew it would be to become involved with Meredith, he *still* wanted her.

What he needed was his head examined.

Giving up any pretense that he'd spend the evening pursuing an uncomplicated few hours of entertainment—with or without female companionship—he pulled on a pair of sweats and a T-shirt from which he'd long ago ripped the sleeves and neck, and laced up his battered running shoes. If he couldn't will thoughts of Meredith out of his brain, maybe he could exhaust them out.

He ran for hours. Until his muscles were screaming and his heart felt like it would explode. His T-shirt stuck to his torso, and sweat ran freely down his temples by the time he turned and headed back to his spacious, very empty apartment.

He rounded the side of the building and stopped short. There, parked beneath the porte cochere, was the silver limo. Meredith's driver must have been on the lookout for Pierce, because he stood beside her door and immediately opened it.

Her foot appeared, the high, thin heel of her shoe seeming to echo the fragility of her slender ankles. Then her calf, and a perfect knee, and her hand as the driver took it and assisted her from the vehicle.

She'd exited cars hundreds of times in just such a manner. There was nothing the least bit overt about her movements. And still, Pierce's blood was surging, his mouth dry, by the time she stood by the car.

The driver stepped away, discreet as ever but always on the watch for the princess's safety. Meredith slowly stepped toward Pierce, her expression uncertain.

He'd done that to her. Made her uncertain. Made her more guarded than she'd ordinarily have reason to be.

He hated it. Even though he knew he'd do the same things over again if he had to, he hated those very things he'd done in his life that separated them.

But he wanted her. He'd always wanted her, and the older they grew, the more often he saw her, the worse it became.

She moistened her lips, and the small, nervous action went straight to his gut. Then she lifted her chin a little. "Is the dinner invitation still open?"

He was a bad case. The invitation in the first place had been inappropriate. The smart course would be to recant. "Yes."

A small glint of pleasure lit her eyes. "Then I accept."

"Get rid of Bobby." It was probably a tactical error on his part, as the driver would assuredly report where he'd left his charge, but Pierce didn't care just then. He saw the way her eyes had gone nervous again and realized what she thought. "I'll get you home tonight."

"I don't know whether to be relieved or disappointed," she murmured. Then smiled wryly and shook her head slightly as she went over to speak to her driver.

The man protested, as Pierce had known he would. He'd be off the guards so fast his head would spin if he hadn't—Pierce would have insured it. The entire responsibility of a personal guard was that he not leave his assignment even if he *was* filling the role of chauffeur. Pierce walked over in time to hear the driver tell Meredith that he'd have to radio for permission. "No offense intended, Your Grace," he said to Pierce, "but I've got to follow my orders."

Pierce nodded. "Colonel," he corrected flatly. "Do what you've got to do. I'll see her home myself."

Meredith's response to it all was resignation. She knew the drill, after all, having lived in a fairly public fishbowl all her life. Pierce held open the door and waited until Meredith went inside. "Call up before you leave," he told Bobby, who nodded and was looking rather satisfied at having an unexpected night off.

Inside the building, Pierce escorted her up to his flat. Neither spoke, but the thick silence was not exactly awkward. Anticipatory, perhaps. He pulled out his key and unlocked the door, pushing it wide.

Meredith could barely drag her eyes from Pierce. She hadn't seen such a display of bare flesh on him in, well, ever. Not even when he'd been seventeen and wielding a hammer on that long-ago summer school project when she'd first met him. She'd known his shoulders were broad—how could she not have noticed that? But in the ragged sleeveless shirt that hung damply against him, she realized that they were roped with long, well-defined muscles. He wasn't brawny and bulging, but hard and smooth and sinewy. His was such a purely masculine beauty that she could barely make her mouth form words when all it wanted to do was hang open.

Realizing that she was standing there like a fool, she stepped past him into his flat. There, at least, she could openly look around.

She realized he was waiting for some comment, and she swallowed. "It's not quite what I expected," she admitted, stepping across the open foyer toward a large, airy great room. So many places in Penwyck were filled with a rabbit's den of small rooms. But not Pierce's place. It fairly soared. To the ceiling above. To the expanse of windows and French doors along one wall.

She heard a soft click and looked over her shoulder to see he'd closed the front door. Silly, but it seemed suddenly intimate, standing there in his foyer. The key pinged when he tossed it into the cut crystal bowl on the foyer table. He stepped around her. "What'd you expect?"

She followed him, moving from the warm mahogany flooring onto thick carpeting the color of cream into which a dribble of coffee had been stirred. She dropped her useless little purse on a long couch upholstered in a sinfully soft butterscotch leather that made her simply want to run her hands over it for the sheer pleasure of it. "Considering your office? Not this."

This was a dream. Contemporary but not cold. Masculine but not utilitarian. And between the three French doors stood beautiful, vividly green potted palms that reached nearly to the top of the door frames.

"I had a decorator come in," he said blandly.

Meredith couldn't imagine doing it any other way, though she knew there were plenty of people who spent hours poring over fabric swatches and paint chips. "You hired the right one," she said faintly.

His lips twitched a little. "I'll tell her so the next time I see her."

Her. Naturally. Jealousy coursed, swift and hot, through Meredith, though she'd roast on a spit before showing it. "You'll have to give me her name," she said blithely, and headed toward one of the French doors.

On the other side of it was a narrow, wrought-iron balcony that ran the length of all the doors. "Do you mind?" She reached for the handle.

"Go ahead. Make yourself at home. I need a shower."

She froze. Of course he'd shower. He'd obviously been running.

"Unless you want to join me." He waited a beat, then laughed, though it didn't sound particularly filled with joviality. "Relax, Your Royal Highness. I'm joking. Go on out. I won't be long."

Her fingers tightened around the handle, and she quickly went out before she succumbed to temptation and followed him to share his shower, whether he was joking or not.

Chapter Ten

"Any place you'd like to particularly go?"

Meredith turned quickly, her hands clutching the wrought iron behind her back. "I didn't hear you come out."

He looked up from the silk tie he'd thrown around his collar but hadn't yet knotted. "Sorry. Didn't mean to startle you. So?"

She watched his fingers work the gray patterned silk. Fascinated. "I've never seen anyone do that."

His eyebrows shot up, and if she wasn't mistaken, a dusky tinge touched his freshly shaven jaw. "You've been around men wearing ties all your life."

"Wearing them, yes," she said, feeling foolish, particularly under the close way he was looking at her. "Oh, never mind."

His jaw ticked, and after a moment, he did something magical, and the knot was perfect, the tie looking nice against the paler gray shirt he wore. In fact, altogether, he looked nice. Not the least bit like the colonel. And very much like the man.

She swallowed. "Must we go out somewhere?"

"Afraid you'll be seen with me?"

She made a face, knowing he wasn't serious. "It'd be more logical if you were afraid of being seen with me, considering all that Jean-Paul went through with Megan."

"Considering that Jean-Paul loves Megan, I doubt he's troubled now by what went on in the tabloids."

"Well, you're not in...in love with me," she said hurriedly, wishing she'd never even suggested they stay in. It was patently obvious he was prepared to go out. Maybe he didn't want to be alone with her.

"I've got steak in the freezer, eggs in the fridge and a box of dried pasta in the cupboard. What's your pleasure?"

Oh, her thoughts were scrambling. "Er, dried pasta?"

He loosened the knot of his tie and walked out of the room. "You've probably never had anything but fresh-made pasta your entire life."

She followed him, looking about, her curiosity as alive as ever. "Nice kitchen. More of the decorator's work?"

"Yes." He pulled open a glass-fronted cabinet and withdrew a blue box that he tossed on the counter. It slid across the slick granite surface and stopped right in front of her. She turned it around to read the label. "Macaroni and cheese."

"It's the ultimate comfort food," he said dryly. "Trust me on this."

"I've had macaroni and cheese before."

"Right."

"Well, I have." She picked up the box and studied it. "I can't quite see how it came from something like this, though."

"From the kitchen at the palace? I'm sure it didn't." He plucked the box from her fingers and set it by the stove before filling a pot with water and plunking it over the flame. "Wine?"

She slid onto one of the bar stools at the island in the center of the enormous room and propped her elbows on the counter. "Yes, please."

He went to the wine rack on the wall between the kitchen and the dining room and slid out a bottle, which he set on the counter in front of her. Then he went to the wide stainless-fronted fridge and pulled out a bottle of beer. He popped it open even as he reached for a corkscrew. Meredith held up her hand, though, as he reached for the wine. "Do you have another beer?"

He looked surprised. But he opened the refrigerator door again and pulled out another bottle. "I'll get you a glass."

"No." She held out her hand for the bottle and twisted off the top when he handed it to her.

"You've done that before."

"Is that so hard to believe? That I've had a beer or two in my life? My friend Lissa Lowell introduced it to me while I was at university. I did go away, you know."

He smiled faintly. "Yes, I know you did. But you

still had a staff and were very carefully chaperoned, living with some distant cousin of the King's, I believe. So, university antics aside, you still seem more the Château Lafite Rothschild sort.''

She laughed a little. "I pinched a bottle of Lafite from the wine cellar for a picnic a few years ago. Nineteen forty-nine. Our cellar master nearly had a stroke.''

His smile died, and he turned to the stove. "I'll bet.''

The water was boiling, and as she watched, he tore open the box and dumped the dried macaroni in, catching a white envelope from going into the water with the pasta, and pitched the empty box in the trash beneath the sink. "Is something wrong?''

"Rothschild,'' he muttered, shaking his head. "I'm boiling macaroni from a bloody box, and you *pinch* a bottle of wine worth more than a thousand dollars for a picnic. Who was it with, anyway?''

"The picnic? Why?'' Her head tilted, and she pushed her hair away from her shoulders. "Jealous?''

"Whomever it was you had a picnic with accompanied by a near-priceless bottle of wine was probably far better company for a princess than I am,'' he said flatly.

Back to that again. Her thumb rubbed over the corner of the label on the bottle. "It was with my sisters, actually. We were celebrating Ana's twenty-first birthday. Just the three of us, with no pomp and circumstance, no servants, no guards, no public relations interference. Just us. We had to be rather creative to accomplish it.''

"So you chose a picnic.''

"Yes. Is it difficult for you to see me on a picnic or something?" She gestured. "Pierce, I think your pot is about to boil over."

He turned to the stove and flipped a knob, lowering the flame. He stuck a wooden spoon into the bubbles and stirred until the frothy boil subsided. "Difficult, no. Unexpected, yes. When you were ten, you were scandalized at the notion of eating off paper plates, much less sitting on the ground without a cloth beneath your royal butt."

"My royal butt was a pain," she admitted ruefully. "I was very much on my high horse that summer. I was trying so hard to emulate my mother, you know." She remembered that summer vividly. How utterly horrid she had behaved. How fascinated by *him* she had been. "I failed miserably, of course. Even now I don't come close to Mother's standard."

He turned off the heat and grabbed a brass colander from the rack of pots over her head. "You are the image of Her Majesty," he said flatly.

"Her Majesty is grace personified," she demurred, watching him drain the macaroni, then dump it back in the pot to which he added a lump of butter and a splash of milk. But when he tore open the white envelope and began sprinkling a vile orange powder into the mixture, her eyes widened. "Pierce?"

He was stirring it all over a low flame. "Yeah."

"Was that orange...substance *cheese?*"

"Yeah."

She smiled weakly. "Oh."

He laughed softly. "You ought to see your face. I believe you had the same expression when you were ten and learned you were expected to not only eat a tuna fish sandwich for lunch off a paper plate while sitting in a circle on the ground with the other school kids, but that you had to help make the sandwich, as well.''

''Your mother handed out can openers to five of us,'' Meredith recalled. ''And cans of tuna to another group. Then she handed around the loaf of bread for us to divide.''

''It was to help the twerps learn teamwork.''

''You were with the older kids. Mostly girls.''

He tilted his head, remembering. ''Yeah.'' His eyelids lowered, giving him a devilish look. ''God bless those teenage girls. It made that summer particularly worthwhile.''

Meredith rolled her eyes. She'd detested the gaggle of girls who'd surrounded him nearly every hour of those days during that summer-long project. ''I didn't know how to use the can opener.''

''So, you could have asked for help instead of pitching a little fit about it.''

''It didn't occur to me that most of my classmates didn't know how to use the things, either. I felt utterly like the odd princess out.'' She smiled faintly. ''I never did learn how to use one.''

''A can opener?'' He turned off the flame once again and opened a cupboard and a drawer. He plunked a can of mandarin oranges on the counter in front of her and handed her a small can opener. ''Give it a go.''

It wasn't the kind of opener that had long handles covered in rubber. In fact, the little metal contraption was small enough to enclose with her fist. She picked it up, turned it over and around in her fingers. ''I thought kitchens were usually equipped with electric can openers. I'm fairly certain that is what is in Chef's kitchen.''

''Stop stalling and open the can.'' He reached over and turned the can opener around so she was holding it correctly. ''Like that. Come on, Your Royal Highness. You're an intelligent woman. You drink beer from the bottle. You can do this, too. Open the can.''

She looked at the label. ''So that we can have little canned oranges to go with the orange cheese stuff.'' She couldn't help smiling.

''We can always go out.''

''No, no. I wouldn't miss this for the world.'' Besides, she was enjoying herself. Immensely. And though she hadn't really known what to expect when she'd asked Bobby to stop at Pierce's building, she wasn't sure she'd expected this much enjoyment to come of it.

She studied the can opener for a moment, then fit it to the edge of the can. The teeth bit, and slowly, she turned the metal handle while squeezing the other two parts together, and managed to open the can of oranges. When she was done, she looked up, feeling triumphant. ''I did it!''

Pierce leaned on the other side of the island counter, his eyes glinting with laughter. ''A well-rounded, talented woman.''

He was so close, she could see the fine web of lines that arrowed out from the corners of his eyes, could see each individual, spiky eyelash that seemed so dark in contrast to his pale, ever changing gaze. And just that suddenly, the ease between them was once again pregnant with tension. "Why did you invite me for dinner?" The words came before she could think.

Those thick, spiky lashes narrowed around his eyes as he watched her closely. "Why did you change your mind and accept?"

"I don't know," she admitted in a low voice. She didn't. She truly did not know what was driving her these days. It troubled her, that inability to figure out her motivation. "Except that maybe *I* couldn't stay away from *you*."

"Well," he said after a moment, "maybe for now it'd be better if we just forgot about reasons."

She slowly reached over the island countertop and handed him the can opener. "Has there been anything in your life that you've done or not done without considering reasons? Or consequences?"

His fingers grazed her palm as he took the can opener and dropped it in the drawer. "Sometimes, Meredith, you've got to just follow your—" he hesitated for a moment, as if searching for the right word "—instincts."

Or follow your heart, she thought. It's what Megan had done with Jean-Paul, and on the day of her wedding, her sister had been about as happy as a woman could be. Maybe that's what had led Meredith to Pierce's door, after all.

She smiled slightly. "I guess we need some plates for that macaroni concoction."

He nodded and straightened. "China or paper?"

"Paper, of course. Just to prove to you that I'm a changed woman from that ten-year-old."

He'd turned and was reaching into an overhead cupboard but looked at her over his shoulder, one eyebrow lifting. "No doubt about that, Your Royal Highness."

He held her gaze far longer than was polite or comfortable, and she felt her cheeks heat. She didn't know why, though. Less than a week ago, she'd practically thrown herself at him, nearly begged him to take her to his bed. Then he was getting out the plates and telling her which drawer to open for the flatware, and she began breathing again.

Despite his comment over paper versus china, it was stoneware, manufactured on Penwyck. And they ate there at the kitchen island, feet propped on the rungs of the wooden bar stools. Macaroni and cheese from a box—which she vowed to pressure Chef into preparing for her at least once a week from now on— beer in the bottle and mandarin oranges they ate out of the can with a fork they shared.

Meredith knew that no matter how long she lived, she would probably never enjoy a meal more.

"Is something wrong with the coffee, darling?" Marissa watched as her eldest child slowly seemed to become aware she'd been asked a question and looked at the small gold spoon. She'd been stirring the coffee for goodness knows how long. It was still very early, and Marissa and Meredith were alone in the breakfast room.

"No." Meredith tapped the spoon once and balanced it on the delicate china saucer. "I guess I'm a little distracted this morning."

Marissa hid her smile by taking a sip of coffee. She thought it a bit strong and made a mental note to ask Chef to switch to the French roast. For some reason,

Morgan had forsaken tea altogether and had lately taken to liking coffee at breakfast. Coffee that was strong enough to melt a spoon, but that didn't mean the rest of them had to suffer. "I'm told you were rather late getting in last night. Or should I say this morning?"

"Mother, I'm hardly a teenager."

"No, you're a grown, very beautiful, highly sought-after woman. But you are still my daughter, and I am concerned about you."

"Concerned?" Meredith laughed faintly. "I had dinner with a friend. We were late getting in. It was nothing."

"That friend happening to be Colonel Prescott."

"Do you have your spies at work again, Mother?"

"Meredith," Marissa chided gently.

"I know." Meredith sighed. She picked up the spoon, adding a drizzle of cream to the coffee and stirred again.

"Darling, you're about to send me insane with that stirring. What is it?"

Meredith stared at the spoon as if she'd never seen it. Set it down. Folded her hands in her lap. "How do you know when you're in love?"

Marissa's eyebrows rose, and a bittersweet pang swept through her. She wanted her children to all find love with the right partner. That didn't mean it was all that easy as a mother to let go when they did. It was a lesson she'd had to begin learning with Megan and Jean-Paul. "Do you think you're in love?"

Meredith picked up the spoon, seemed to realize it and set it down. "He makes me crazy."

"That's a start," she said humorously.

"When did you know you were in love with Father?"

Marissa went still for a moment. She set down her coffee. "Darling, your father and I had an arranged marriage."

"I know, but you did fall in love." Meredith didn't seem to question it.

"Yes," Marissa said softly. "I did fall in love with your father." Surprisingly easily. But then Morgan had been handsome, powerful, charismatic. Giving him five children had been Marissa's joy. But had Morgan ever fallen in love with her? Thirty-five years of marriage ought to have given her the answer to that. Yet it hadn't. And even after thirty-five years, she sometimes felt very much as if she were married to a stranger.

"How did you know?" Meredith asked again.

"I looked at him one day and knew it was so," Marissa said simply.

"Why? Was there something special about the day? Something you were doing together to make you realize it?"

Marissa studied her daughter. "You always were one to pick apart every situation so you could better understand it. You're very much like His Majesty in that respect."

"And?"

"We were doing nothing special," Marissa said gently. "Goodness, darling, I can't recall even *what* we were doing or where we were. But I do remember very clearly looking at him and simply knowing it. *I love this man,* I thought." She watched Meredith for a moment. "Love doesn't always arrive with a clash of cymbals and waving flags. With pounding hearts and mouths gone dry. Sometimes it just seeps into you, barely noticed at first, until you realize your soul has become filled right up to overflowing with it and you can no longer remember a time when you didn't feel that way.''

"He didn't even kiss me good-night," Meredith murmured, and Marissa stifled another smile as her daughter's cheeks colored. "We spent the entire evening together. He took a shower, fixed dinner—"

"Took a shower?"

"He'd been out running," Meredith said absently. "After dinner, we sat in his living room and…"

Marissa sipped the dreadful coffee for courage. "And what?"

"Talked. Well—" Meredith's eyes narrowed in thought "—we talked mostly about me. And business at the RII. The alliances. Everyone is working madly to nail the negotiations. I think he was quite exhausted, actually, though he'd never admit it. He doesn't say much about himself. Ever. Have you noticed that?"

"Your father has a particularly high respect for Colonel Prescott," Marissa said. "I believe he's a good man. But I cannot claim to particularly understand him."

"That makes two of us." Meredith pressed her palms against the table and rose. "He loathes it when someone makes a point of his nobility, you know. In his mind he is a military man first, last and always. Not a duke. I can't quite figure out why."

"For someone who doesn't understand a man, you've certainly keyed into something."

Meredith shook her head, looking discouraged. "He makes no secret of it. I know he doesn't neglect his duties to Aronleigh, but he really has a bug about it." She shrugged. "That was it for the evening. We had a nice time, but I doubt there will be a repeat. Not only does he detest his own title, but he has an issue about mine, and frankly, trying to figure him out makes my heart hurt."

"Your...heart, dear?"

"My head. I meant my head."

"Of course you did."

"So why should I spend any more of my time thinking about this? I've plenty on my plate as it is with my public engagements, not to mention my other duties at the RII. I've seen enough of Colonel Prescott in the past several days to last me quite a while, thank you."

Her daughter nodded decisively, as if she could control her emotions that easily. Marissa, however, knew better. She'd had thirty-five years of schooling in the confusing art of love, the pain of secrets and the necessity of learning that not everything in life was plainly black and white.

She picked up her coffee, smiling softly, unaware of the tinge of sadness in the smile. "Of course, darling. Anything you say."

Chapter Eleven

"And so—" Meredith smiled at the gathered crowd "—on behalf of my family and the entire country of Penwyck who owe a debt of gratitude for the service these men have given to us, it is my very great pleasure to announce the opening of Sunquest, North Shore's own residential care facility for retired military personnel." She held up the oversize clippers and snipped through the red, blue and gold ribbon that had been whipping in the brisk breeze where it was strung across the front of the brand-new building.

The guests clapped, a few whistled, low thunder rolled overhead, and Meredith's smile felt strained.

She hadn't known Pierce would be present at the dedication ceremony. His name hadn't been on the list she'd been given earlier that day when the King had unexpectedly asked Meredith to take his place at the event. If his dark expression was anything to go by, Pierce hadn't expected her to be there in the King's stead, either.

If she'd been confused by him before, now she was even more so.

She'd barely finished speaking with the directors and other powers that be of the institution when Pierce came up to her, wrapping his hand around her upper arm and drawing her away. "Where is he?"

Meredith frowned. Anger seemed to radiate from him. "Who?"

He drew her farther from the other people until they were practically around the corner of the building. "Your father," he said under his breath. "Where is he?"

"Well, heavens, Pierce, I don't know." She tugged her hair back when the wind caught it. "I assumed it was something to do with the alliances. His office notified me something had come up that required his attention, so I came in his stead. What's the problem? It's not the first time I've stood in for him at a public engagement."

"It's the first time I haven't been informed," he said evenly. "I have to make some calls. Don't go anywhere."

She didn't even have a chance to ask where she would go since she'd dismissed her driver—Pierce was already striding away.

Meredith sighed. Every day that brought the alliances closer to completion meant one day more of tension for the parties involved. Not that there was much time for her to dwell on it, for the administrator and one of his staff physicians approached her and said the new residents inside were ready to greet her. They began on the third floor. Dr. Herrold had eyed her with some surprise when she'd insisted on meeting every patient who was willing to meet her. He quickly turned over the task to his associate, who'd been trailing behind them.

"I thought he'd never leave." Lissa Lowell grinned at Meredith the moment the administrator left them alone.

"Dr. Lowell." Meredith grinned back. "I thought I'd never have a chance to speak with you."

Her old college chum shrugged. "Herrold likes the glory and he's a great administrator, but he's not much for dealing with the individual patients. May I just say you look terrific? I saw Colonel Prescott whispering in your ear right after the ribbon cutting. He's dishy. Sort of brooding, but *very* dishy."

Meredith laughed wryly. Brooding was right. Dishy was accurate, but a little too fluffy a word in her opinion. "We'll have to get together and have lunch," she told Lissa. "Soon. There's so much to catch up on. I still can't believe you've settled in Penwyck. You were all set to move to the United States."

"My fiancé lives here," Lissa said simply, squeezing Meredith's hand. "I wish you could make it tomorrow afternoon, though."

Meredith had received the invitation for the luncheon shower that was being thrown for the couple. "My schedule was already set," she said. "I wish I could make it, too. I want to meet this man you threw over America for."

Lissa smiled understandingly. Then she got down to business, introducing Meredith to each and every patient. It was some time before they made it through the second and first floors and down to the main level where the recreation area was located.

Meredith immediately spotted Pierce in conversation with a trio of elderly men sitting at a table over cards, but Lissa was drawing her over to another small group, all of whom were seated in wheelchairs. She introduced each man, and as they got to the last, Meredith looked at him. "Major Fox," she exclaimed. "My goodness, what a pleasure." From the corner of her eye, she saw Lissa reach for her pager and with a quick wave darted toward the elevator.

The man beamed at Meredith, looking far more elderly than she knew he must be. "Your Royal Highness, I didn't think you'd remember an old face like mine." His voice was raspy, his skin paper white. A folded plaid blanket was draped across his knees, and he looked so thin that a dash of breeze might blow through him.

"Of course I remember." She pulled up a folding chair and sat down with the men. "You were the guard at the side gate for as long as I could remember." She smiled, including the other men. "He always winked at my brothers and sisters and me behind our parents' backs whenever we entered the palace."

"And you snuck me blueberry muffins from the kitchen on Sunday mornings before you went out for church."

Meredith laughed softly even as her heart broke a little for the man. It had been softhearted Megan who'd done the sneaking, not Meredith. "I think Chef thought Old Pierre was sneaking in from the gardens when he wasn't looking and pinching the muffins in exchange for the blooms Megan would sneak from the garden and leave for Chef.'' She sighed, shaking her head. ''Those were the days.''

The other men guffawed. ''Listen to the lassie,'' one said. ''As if she's so decrepit.''

Meredith chuckled. ''But Major Fox, you retired when I went away to university and I'd heard you'd gone to Majorco to live with your son.''

The major nodded, making his oxygen tube jiggle slightly. ''That I did. Didn't much care for the boy's wife, though. No sense of humor.'' He shrugged his thin shoulders. ''Penwyck's my home. Born here. I'll die here.''

Meredith reached over and clasped his hand gently, careful to avoid the IV taped to his thin wrist. ''It's good to see you again,'' she said softly.

He smiled, looking weak and shaky enough that she worried he shouldn't be sitting in the chair. ''The colonel's got eyes for ye, girl.''

''Excuse me?''

''The colonel. He's over there looking this way, prob'ly expectin' me to be telling you what a hero he is.''

Meredith looked over her shoulder to see that Pierce was, indeed, watching them.

''I remember when he wasn't much more'n a whelp,'' one of the other men said.

Meredith's smile widened at the thought of anyone calling Pierce a whelp. She still held the major's hand, and she squeezed it lightly. ''Stories? You've got stories? Oh, lovely.''

Two of the men nudged each other with their el-

bows and laughed uproariously. "Stories are about all
we got these days, miss. Er, begging your pardon,
Your Royal Highness."

Meredith wanted to hug them all, they were so
friendly and genuine. She sat, enthralled, as the small
group told story after story, each one more outlandish
than the next as they tried to outdo each other. Her
sides ached from laughing at the antics they re-
counted.

Though not all the stories were funny, as she heard
about sons and daughters. Families who came and
went. And as they talked, she noticed that Major
Fox's attention wandered. Sometimes talking as if he
were actually back in those days, sometimes very
much here in the present.

"I'm sorry about your brother, Your Majesty," he
said, obviously mistaking her for her mother. "But it
was a bad night in Penwyck, ye see. So confused."

"Majorco," Meredith murmured softly. "Edwin
died in Majorco."

Major Fox frowned, his eyes vague. "Majorco? My
son is in Majorco."

"Yes."

His eyes were tearing, and she felt like crying right
along with him. "You were so kind when my wife
died last year, Your Majesty. I'll never forget that.
And His Majesty, helping me move to Majorco. I
hadn't been there since we took—"

"Major Fox."

Meredith nearly jumped out of her skin when
Pierce spoke behind her. She went still as a mouse
when he rested his hand on her shoulder as he greeted
the other men.

"You want to know the story, Your Royal Highness," Major Fox said suddenly, once more looking perfectly lucid. "You ought to be asking the colonel. He saved my life that awful night. Remember it clear as a bell." He nodded, then frowned and began muttering about cats getting into his garden.

Dr. Herrold signaled an attendant, but before the young man could wheel away Major Fox, Meredith leaned over and kissed the man's papery cheek. "That's for all those winks over the years," she whispered, and he patted her head as if she were still a child.

"Gentlemen," Pierce addressed the remaining residents, "I hope you'll forgive me for stealing away Her Highness, but she has another engagement this evening so I need to return her to Marlestone."

Meredith looked at him, hiding her surprise. She finished her goodbyes, made a point of speaking with Dr. Herrold about Major Fox's accommodations, then joined Pierce at the door. "*You* need to return me to Marlestone?"

He closed his hand over her elbow and escorted her from the building. "Herrold told me that you were intending to borrow a car to drive back. What happened to your driver? There was no report that he'd left you here unattended."

"You make me sound as if I'm the child Major Fox still thinks I am. I don't need to be attended to, you know."

"Poor choice of words," he said. Their footsteps crunched over the gravel drive as he headed toward an aging convertible. He opened the door for her and rounded the car, sliding behind the wheel and starting the engine with an annoyed look. "You can't go around dismissing your driver, Meredith. It's not safe. He's the closest thing to a bodyguard you've got right now."

"Oh, please, Pierce. Penwyck has one of the lowest crime rates in the world."

"And you're a jewel in the crown of Penwyck, not an ordinary citizen."

She shook her head. "There's not a person out there with reason to harm me or my family."

"It wouldn't be the first time."

Her eyebrows lifted. "Excuse me?"

"Security is tightening every day the signing of the alliances grows closer. You know that. What on earth possessed you to let Bobby go for the day?"

"Because it is his son's first birthday today. Having him drive me about the country when he should be at home with his family was ludicrous. And I'd like an explanation of that comment!" Her voice rose as the tires bit over the gravel.

"So why didn't he call it in? The guards would have had somebody else out here to replace him in an hour."

"He *did* call, because I heard him. But Dr. Herrold kindly offered his help when he overheard Bobby's protests, and I said there was no point in sending another car out for me. I made the decision, and that's all there was to it. And since when has my family not been safe going about our business in the usual manner? Are there some intelligence reports that are saying otherwise?"

"Any royal has to be concerned with personal security," he said flatly. "I was speaking generally."

She was thoroughly irritated and certain he wasn't telling her the entire story. "Well, then, what's this about another engagement I have that necessitated my leaving so abruptly? I had Lillian clear my schedule when I had to stand in on this appointment." She thought about the one engagement Lillian hadn't canceled with George Valdosta, and her conscience niggled when she deliberately didn't mention it. She wanted to know what was on Pierce's mind.

"The engagement is with me."

Her jaw dropped delicately, all other irritations vanishing like a puff of cotton caught in the rushing wind. "Indeed. For what, exactly?"

His lips twisted. "Your enthusiasm flatters me."

"Now that's the pot calling the kettle black," she retorted, gathering her long hair in her hand. It would be a dreadful mess from blowing in the convertible by the time they made it to Marlestone. But she so enjoyed the open air, which smelled a little like the rain that had not yet joined the clouds or the thunder, that she didn't even consider asking him to put up the top. Instead, she opened her tiny purse and pulled out a gold clip, which she shoved into her hair to keep it somewhat contained. "And, as it happens," she said firmly, "I've decided not to see you anymore."

His glance at her was amused. "That's what we've been doing, is it? *Seeing* each other?"

"What would you call it?" They were leaving North Shore behind and heading along the narrow road that would take them through the highest mountains on the island. The road was well maintained, but it was very curvy, necessitating slower speeds. He drove well, his hands capable on the wheel. Everything about him was capable.

She looked away, thinking that she'd been listening too much to Anastasia lately.

"How about deliberately running into each other?"

She sighed faintly, not wanting to admit to even the slightest bit of amusement. "You're a complicated man, Colonel Prescott."

"Not particularly. I'm about as ordinary as they come."

She tilted her chin, eyeing him. "You're joking, right?"

"My mother was a schoolteacher. My father a minister. There was little money for university because pretty much everything they made went into the church, so I joined the army and got my schooling there."

"Just a simple man," she murmured dryly. "Who ended up a colonel in that army, a member of the RET and the Duke of Aronleigh. Very simple." His lips twisted, but he remained silent. "So, how *did* you save Major Fox's life? Was it before he became a guard at the palace? Except I can't remember a time from my childhood when he wasn't assigned to the palace."

That, at least, merited a response. "Fox has Alzheimer's disease," he said. "He was confused."

"Only part of the time. Are you saying you didn't save his life?" She figured it was more likely than not that Pierce had directly saved lives over the course of his military career. The King wouldn't have awarded the man a vast dukedom for nothing, after all. But as Pierce's area of expertise was intelligence, he knew that, by necessity, most details of his career were particularly secure.

He didn't answer.

"It's very beautiful through here," she said, deciding that it was prudent, for now, to change the subject rather than pursue her hunch that the shadows in Pierce's eyes had something to do with Major Fox. "I've always liked it in the mountains."

He shot her a quick look as if he didn't quite trust her easy retreat. "I grew up near here."

"I know." She tucked back a lock that had escaped her clip. "What *is* the event this evening?"

Pierce wished he hadn't fallen back on that excuse to get Meredith away from Fox. Now he had to come up with something, and the something he wanted was the something he always wanted.

Him. Her. Together.

"I have to attend a dinner party," he finally said. "For the base."

"A dinner party that requires my attendance?" She crossed her arms, obviously piqued. "Can't you simply ask me out in any semblance of a normal fashion?"

"I tried that the other evening at the library."

"No, actually, what you did that evening was more in the form of a demand. 'Have dinner with me.'" She mimicked his low voice.

"You enjoyed it well enough."

"True," she admitted.

Pierce knew it had to be his imagination that he could hear the soft rasp of her silk-clad legs as she slowly crossed them. The wind was blowing around them, and the car engine was loud, so hearing such a

soft sound was impossible. A logical reasoning tha
did nothing to keep his senses from believing wha
they wanted. It didn't help that her skirt was shorte
than usual today. When she crossed those long
shapely legs, the charcoal gray fabric rode up above
her knees.

She had beautiful knees. *She* was beautiful.

"Who is going to be there?"

He harshly marshaled his thoughts and named a
few of his senior officers.

"And their wives."

"Yes. They've made reservations in Sterling."
That, at least, was true. Though they'd be mighty sur
prised when he showed up with a woman. This
woman in particular, as he'd never made any bone
that he preferred not to socialize with the Penwycks

She'd gone silent again, making him wonder wha
was ticking along inside her brain. "This is simply a
social thing, then," she finally said.

"Yes."

"And you want *me* to go. With you. Together."

"Yes. Dammit, Meredith, what is so hard to un
derstand about it?"

She held up her hand. "After the evening at Ho
rizons, you made it plain that you didn't want to pur
sue a, um, a relationship with me." She ticked of
one finger. "Deliberately proven when you drove me
home last Friday night with hardly a good-night de
spite the fact that we seemed to have had an enjoyable
evening together." She ticked off another finger
"And mostly because you've never wanted me any
where with you that wasn't an official event. Not even
then, really. And certainly not in public."

"There's a first for everything, isn't there."

He felt, more than saw, her look at him, her mouth opening, but the engine suddenly spit, and steam rolled from beneath the hood. Swearing under his breath, he steered to the side of the road as far as he could near the stone barrier. "Get out of the car."

"I didn't take studies in auto mechanics, either."

"Considering the narrowness of the road, if the car gets hit, better that you're not inside it, don't you think?" He climbed out and raised the hood, frowning at it, then at her when she came to stand beside him.

"Can you fix it, Doctor?"

"Have you always been such a smart-mouthed miss?"

She seemed to ponder that. "Unfortunately, I fear I have. It tends to scare off most men."

"That why you're still a virgin? You go around deliberately scaring off most men? What's the deal, anyway? I know for a fact that Dr. Waltham has had you on birth control pills for years."

Her jaw dropped, and her cheeks went red. "Well, Pierce, you certainly know how to stop a conversation."

"I also know you had antibiotics a few years back and saw a chiropractor for a while when you took a tumble from your horse when you returned from university. And that, on the whole, you're unusually healthy."

"Such important matters for Intelligence," she murmured, refusing to be any more embarrassed than she already was. "And the birth control is to, um, regulate things, if you must know."

He nodded, seeming not in the least bit fazed by the utterly private matter.

"Though, frankly—" she sounded piqued "—if you know so many personal details about me, it's a wonder you didn't already know about my stellar love life."

"I know about your health care. The rest was your business. But you've been giving me enough hints, Your Royal Highness, to get the gist."

"Oh, no." She shook her head. "None of that. Not while we're discussing my, er, my…"

"Virginity," he supplied. "It's not a dirty word. You can say it." Frankly, he'd been surprised when it had finally dawned on him. Surprised and unexpectedly moved. He'd never been one to take someone's innocence, yet he was aware there was a damnable satisfaction deep inside him that no other man had touched her that way.

"My *decision*," she said deliberately, "to not sleep around. Which, in any case, is none of your business."

He saw the broken hose and knew he had nothing on hand to fix it. Which meant they had a walk in store. He could handle it. But Meredith's sexy shoes would be another story. "Then why did you make it a point of hinting around about it?"

"I think there's an oxymoron in there somewhere."

"I think you suspect I'm not scared off so easily."

Her lips pursed and her eyebrows shot up. "Colonel, I seriously doubt there is anything at all that scares you, least of all me."

He ran his gaze over her, settling, catching hers. "That's where you are wrong, Meredith. Because you are the one thing in this world that does scare me."

Chapter Twelve

She was staring at him as if he'd lost his head.

Obviously, he had.

He pushed down the hood until it latched and wondered what would have happened if he'd let nature take its course between Meredith and Major Fox. Pierce's father had always warned that truths could never remain hidden forever. "I'm sorry. There's nothing I can do with this. We've got to walk. I'd call for assistance, but the cell won't work up in the mountains."

She seemed as eager to forget what he'd just said as he was. "Then we walk. At least it's not raining."

"Yet." He looked at the threatening clouds. When the storm hit, it would be a devil of one.

She reached over the side of the car and pulled out her little square of a purse. "I'm ready."

There she stood. The princess dressed in gray silk and sky-high heels, her long brown hair contained in a tumble of waves by a thin gold clasp. And he, an unwilling duke with grease on his hands and blood on his soul.

A more unlikely or ill-advised pairing he couldn't begin to imagine. No matter what, though, he still seemed to head right down that path.

He waited for her to join him, making sure he walked between her and the road, on the off chance a car did pass. They headed in the direction from which they'd come.

He kept his pace slower than usual to accommodate her spiky heels, though she made no complaint. They'd been walking for quite a while when she finally broke the silence. "I might point out," she said rather breathlessly, "that had I driven the car Dr. Herrold offered, we might not be in this situation."

"*You* might not be," he agreed. "But that hose would've broken whether you were with me or not."

"Ah." She smiled faintly. "But if I'd been driving the other car, I would have taken this route. As such, there would have been at least *one* car on this dratted road to come by and rescue you."

"Nobody's ever spoken about rescuing me. It's usually the other way around."

She wobbled when her foot slid on a stone, and caught his arm, steadying herself. "Maybe it's time someone did rescue you," she said softly.

Her eyes were serious, and Pierce suddenly wasn't at all certain they were still talking about incapacitated cars. They'd come to a fork in the main road, and he guided her toward the smaller road.

"Where will this take us?"

He looked up the unpaved road that was nearly overgrown with grass and let out a long breath. He took her hand in his and headed forward. "Home."

Home, Meredith soon learned, meant his parent's home. The small cottage they'd shared with their only son. Her feet were positively throbbing, and as soon as he unlocked the front door and ushered her inside, she slipped out of her shoes, certain she'd never wear high heels again. "You've kept your parents' place all these years? Do you come here often?"

"Not enough. Obviously," he added as he dashed away a cobweb before she could step into it. "I don't know why I hold on to the place, when it comes right down to it."

She knew. He'd kept the house and property because it had been his parents' home. His home. It was sentimental, and she knew he'd deny it if she said a single word to that effect. So she didn't. Realizing it was enough.

Pierce went through the small living room, turning on lamps as he went. "Sit. I'll get you something to drink."

Despite her sore feet, she had no desire to sit and an insatiable desire to see every inch of the home in which he'd grown up, so she followed him to the small kitchen where he was filling a glass at the tap.

He handed it to her. "Do you *ever* follow instructions?"

"Not when they come in the form of orders from you," she said with a sweet smile.

"I've noticed that. Nobody gives you orders."

"Not even my father."

"Maybe he ought to have."

"He prefers a rousing debate with me, if the truth be known. Besides, I thought we agreed that I'm not the spoiled girl I once was."

"Yes. Now you're an intractable woman."

"Because I let Bobby off for the afternoon? Because I didn't sit when you said to do so? Please, Pierce, you would be bored stiff with an agreeable little woman who jumped to your every bidding." She decided she was heading down a dangerous road and quickly lifted the water glass.

"Well," he said after a moment, looking as if he were laughing at himself, "you definitely don't *bore* me stiff."

Her gaze immediately flickered over him, and realizing it, she flushed and headed into the living room after hastily finishing the water. There was a piano there, with framed photographs crammed on the top, and she stopped, peering at each one. The largest was a photograph of a young Pierce in his army uniform flanked by his parents. "You look like your father," she murmured, picking up the frame.

"That was taken the summer before they died."

She glanced back and caught the expression that flitted across his face. "You miss them."

He didn't answer that directly. "You remember my mother?"

"Of course I do." She'd been slender, very tall and very blond, with a ready laugh and a gentle word for her students. "I'm sorry that I never met your father."

"He was a tough old man," Pierce mused. "He

didn't take kindly to my enlisting. He wanted me to follow in his footsteps.''

"The Reverend Pierceson Prescott," Meredith murmured.

"Yeah." He ran his hand over his jaw, then through his close-cropped hair. "I thought about it."

"Really." She swallowed the jolt of pleasure that he'd actually shared something personal with her.

"You look surprised. What's the matter? I'm not pious enough for you?"

"Oh, Pierce. Relax your jaw," Meredith chided gently as she carefully set the picture frame into place. "I don't think anything of the sort. It *is* hard for me to picture you having any career other than the military, though. It's such a part of who you are. Just as I know at the center of you is a man of great faith."

He set his glass of water down with a thunk. "How would you know that? *I* don't know that," he muttered.

He was serious, and her heart broke a little. She touched his arms, feeling the warmth and strength of him through the sleeves of his khaki-beige uniform. "Pierce, honor practically oozes from your pores. And what is at the base of honor, if not faith in a greater power?"

He caught her hands in his, enfolding them tightly. "I believe in doing the job," he said flatly. "Honor has no part of it."

She sucked at her lower lip for a moment. "I don't believe that. You're so much more than the job. Why do you refuse to see it?"

"You don't know anything about me."

"I told my mother just about that very same thing the other morning." She quickly slid her fingers around his wrists, reversing the hold when he suddenly let go of her. "I was wrong," she said urgently. "You see, there are some things I *do* know about you. I know that you command respect simply by entering a room. Not because your men and women fear you, but because they trust you. Your political judgments are rock solid, your economic and strategic wisdom immense, or the King would never have asked you to be part of the Royal Elite Team.

"I know you can be dangerously fierce when the situation calls for it, and I know you can be gentle and incredibly sweet, particularly with little girls who've dumped their ice cream on their toes."

"Meredith—"

"No, let me finish. Please?"

"Could I stop you?"

"Probably not," she admitted. "When I get something in my head—"

"You're relentless."

"I think I'll choose to take that as a compliment."

"If you must."

She let out a little laugh, dropping her forehead to his chest for a moment before looking at him again. "See? This is what we end up doing. We dance around each other. And while, when it comes to verbal sparring, I'd rather do it with you than anyone else, I think we fall into that easy habit rather than deal with the more difficult issue of what we feel. Of what we *could* feel, if we let ourselves."

"Meredith, you don't want to know what I feel."

"Yes," she countered fiercely, "I do. That's *all* I

want, practically. I can't sleep at night because of
you. I can't focus on my work like I used to because
of you. I thought, after that day at Horizons, that no
matter what was between us, we were going to go
back to generally avoiding one another. But then you
kept showing up. We kept running into each other.
And I think—no, I *know* you find it as impossible to
go back to that limbo between us as I do.''

"Pardon my bluntness, Your Royal Highness, but
that's lust talking between us.''

"That may be part of it,'' she agreed, feeling her
cheeks grow hot. "I want you, Colonel. I've been
painfully miserable at hiding it, lately. And I know
you want me, whether you like admitting it or not.
I'm not *that* naive. But if lust was all it was, then
we'd have slept together long ago and been done with
it. And you wouldn't have told me not one hour ago
that I scare you.''

"It is just sex.''

She knew him better than that. "Is it? What are
you really afraid of here, Pierce? How could I possibly hurt you?''

He shrugged off her hands and grabbed his water
glass, but he didn't drink. "I told you before. I'll end
up hurting you.''

"Why?''

"Men don't dally with royal princesses,'' he said
flatly. "Particularly virginal ones.''

Her face flamed. "I hate to tell you this, but I really
don't believe you're the dallying sort, either. And
don't bother telling me it's because you're afraid my
daddy will come tearing after you with a shotgun if
he finds you've sullied his little girl.''

"He doesn't need a shotgun," he said blandly. "I believe there is a guillotine somewhere around the palace."

She blew out an impatient laugh, throwing up her hands. "You know, Pierce, if you'd ever just open up about whatever it is that puts those dark shadows in your eyes, maybe you'd find it in you to enjoy life a little."

"Does anyone else know what an active imagination you have?"

"Stop dismissing this."

"Stop making more of it than it is."

"Is it something to do with you being awarded the dukedom? You've never been comfortable with—"

"Hell. You're worse'n a dog with a bone." He shoved the glass on the piano and plowed his hand through her hair, dragging her onto her toes and planting his mouth on hers.

She swayed, fingers digging into his hard shoulders, and gasped when he let her up for air. "A dog? You're the one who...mmm." He kissed her again.

Her knees went weak. Her head fell back. His mouth burned over her cheek, her jaw, her earlobe. "Enlightened...women," she gasped breathlessly, "do not appreciate the Neanderthal approach." Her eyelids felt impossibly heavy all of a sudden, and some meager portion of her brain was aware that she was trembling wildly.

She turned her head, trying to find his mouth, but he eluded her, laughing softly, triumphantly, just like the Neanderthal he was, when she twisted her fingers in his short hair and pulled, dragging his mouth to hers with a demanding cry.

He'd said they were going home. He'd meant his parents' home. She couldn't help but think, though, when he finally capitulated—not with the hot, hungry kiss she'd expected, but with such softness, such exquisite, unexpected tenderness—that kissing him, being in his arms, was where the real home was.

Her palm slid to his jaw, her eyes filling. She knew he'd pull away, he always did. And she wanted to savor the moment. Savor the whisper-soft caress of his lips over hers, the pump of his heartbeat against her breast.

Yes, she wanted to feel his skin against hers. She wanted to be his in all the ways that could mean. But she wanted more than to share their bodies. She wanted to share what was in his head. In his heart.

Then he bent, and she caught her breath when he swept her into his arms. She grabbed his shoulders. "Pierce?"

His eyes were dark. Dangerous. "I want you. More than I've ever wanted anyone in my life. But I am telling you. *Nothing* will come of this. I'd have your innocence, and you'd have nothing. I could take you to bed and we could stay there for a month of Sundays. But that would be it. That's all it will ever be. Is that what you want? Is that *all* you want?"

Her heart clutched as he carried her to the small chintz-covered couch and settled her on it. Her heart climbed into her throat.

She'd danced with heads of state, dined with the rich, the famous and the beautiful. She'd debated with scholars and she'd adroitly avoided proposals from billionaire oil magnates.

She'd never been so unsure of herself as she was

at that moment. "Because you don't feel anything beyond that for me?"

He stepped away from the couch, arms akimbo, head bowed. She could see the tendons in his neck, the sinews in his forearms where he'd rolled up his shirtsleeves. A muscle in his jaw worked.

She sat on the edge of the aging, too-soft couch, afraid if she stood her shaking legs wouldn't support her.

"Yes." He gritted the word. "That's all I feel."

She closed her eyes for a moment, absorbing the dull pain that rolled over her until she thought she could bear it without weeping. Only then did she open her eyes and look at him. Truly look at him. Only then did she see the way he held himself. As if he were hovering on the edge of a cliff. Too still. Too controlled.

Perhaps she was making a fool of herself. Perhaps it was just as he said. But, just possibly, her instincts were dead-on. "I don't believe you."

His head went back, his lips twisting. "You think I'm lying."

"Through your very tightly clenched teeth."

"Fine," he said flatly. "Think whatever the hell you want to think. I'm going to take care of the car. You can wait here."

She expected him to go to the telephone, which sat in plain view on top of a curious little triangular table beside a striped chair. But he strode through the kitchen, and she heard the distinctive sound of a door.

She hurriedly slipped into her shoes and followed. Outside the kitchen was a detached garage across the small patch of yard that was neatly groomed and a rose garden that wasn't. One garage door was open, and she peered into the gloom. He'd switched on a bare overhead bulb, and she was surprised at the neatness inside. In addition to the lawn-care equipment and an assortment of storage boxes stacked on metal shelves, there was a motorcycle that looked fairly new.

Pierce stood at the rear of the garage, pawing through a drawer that she soon realized was part of an elaborate tool chest. ''You're going to fix it yourself?''

He tossed some tools and a few incomprehensible looking items into a canvas bag. ''That's the plan. I'd call for a car but the phone is disconnected.'' He crossed the strap over his shoulder and went to the motorcycle, rocking it forward over the stand and rolling it from the garage before swinging his leg over it. ''Wait inside the house. Please,'' he added before she could open her mouth. ''I shouldn't be long.''

''I thought I wasn't supposed to be left unprotected,'' she said sweetly.

''Meredith, right now, you're safer away from me than you are with me.'' He started the motorcycle and roared around the house and down the road before she could think of a single thing to say in response to that.

She looked at the garage for a moment, wondering if she should close the door, but left it. There were no other houses in the immediate area, and it was obviously not a well-traveled road, considering the length of the grass that was growing over it.

She wandered through the garden, absently pinching off withering blooms the way old Pierre had taught her to do when she was little, traipsing around behind him in the gardens with her curious mind in full gear. Her curiosity now had her wondering why Pierce—for it was likely he—had made an effort at keeping his parents' home in order but had neglected the roses, which had nearly run wild.

The heels of her shoes sank into the soft earth, but she barely noticed. She stood among the overgrown roses, surrounded by tall pines. The air was cooling because of the coming rain, the breeze filled with the heady scent of roses and the tang of evergreen and the kind of silence that was practically deafening.

Then it hit her.

She was totally and completely alone.

There were no servants within earshot, no staff merely the buzz of an intercom away, no royal guards watching for...whatever.

A sharp crack of thunder made her jump, and she deliberately shrugged off the shivers that rippled up and down her spine.

She looked at the overcast gray sky. "It's been a very odd day," she said aloud.

And when she went inside the cozy little house where Pierce had spent his childhood, she wished, in the silliest of ways, that he would hurry back.

Chapter Thirteen

Pierce went into the house through the kitchen door, which was why he saw the mess first. Not a mess, really. But there was a pot in the sink, a crumpled towel on the tiled countertop.

"Meredith?"

She didn't answer, and he shoved his hand through his hair, scattering rainwater as he strode rapidly through the kitchen into the living room. "Mere—" He stopped short, her name dying in his lips.

She was curled up on the sofa, her hands folded together beneath her cheek.

She was asleep.

He blew out a short, relieved breath. Then he realized there were other small differences in the house aside from the stuff in the kitchen. He smelled furniture wax instead of mustiness. And flowers. There was a glass bowl of cut roses sitting in the center of the small round table where he'd eaten meals and done homework. Also sitting on the polished surface were two plates, flatware, glasses, napkins. And in a covered bowl, macaroni and cheese.

"You're back."

He turned on his heel and looked at her. She hadn't moved, and her eyes looked soft with sleep. "It took longer than I thought," he said. But nowhere near long enough to drive out the want burning inside him.

He watched her slowly straighten her legs like a cat stretching in the sun. Point her toes, flex. She'd removed her jacket, and the skirt beneath had climbed another precious inch above her knees. The silver colored blouse she wore looked to him like little more than silky lingerie.

She sat up and tugged the clip from her hair, which cascaded around her shoulders. "I hope you don't mind," she said in a hushed tone. "I tried my hand at cooking."

"And cleaning." His voice sounded strangled. "You shouldn't have."

She looked stricken, unnecessarily reminding him how unique she was. Intelligence and grace with an overwhelmingly appealing innocence that he knew for a fact she revealed very rarely.

"I didn't mean to offend—"

"You didn't." He rubbed his hand over his rib cage, leaving a streak of grease.

She stood, and the hem of her skirt slid down, jealously guarding the two inches of taut leg above her knees from his eyes. "You're wet." She blinked again, giving him an agonizing idea of how she'd awaken in the mornings. Warm and soft and sexily off balance until she fully roused.

"The storm finally hit."

"It's been threatening to all day. Did you get the car going?"

"Anxious to leave?"

Her lashes swept down for a long moment, and when they lifted, all signs of sleepiness were gone. "Do you want me to lie to you or tell the truth?"

One of them was doing enough lying for them both. But he knew the truth, could see it in her eyes, and it was killing him that he was hurting her at all. "It's fixed, but I don't know how long it'll last. The parts I had on hand weren't quite right. I hope it'll get us at least to the base without breaking down again."

"We'll need to get your motorcycle back here?"

"Yeah. I'm sorry, this day is taking a hell of a lot longer than it should have."

She walked to the table, giving him a wide berth. "It's too bad the phone is out. I could have canceled my plans this evening and gotten some work done."

"The telephone's been disconnected for years," he said. "I'm not up here often enough to need a phone." And what had her plans involved, he wondered. Though he didn't make the mistake of suggesting she join him for dinner again. Considering what had transpired between them, it would be foolishness of mammoth proportions.

"But you're up here just often enough to make sure the grounds are groomed," she observed, tongue-in-cheek.

"Yard work can be hired out, Your Royal Highness." And it often was, though not on a regular basis.

"Right. What about the rosebushes, then?"

"What about them?"

"They need tending, too. Can't your hired gardening service take care of your mother's roses, as well?"

"My father's. He was the rose person. Mom was the mechanic."

"Your father's, then. They've nearly gone wild."

"He used to be out there working with them while I'd play ball." The truth was, Pierce couldn't stand to touch the roses. Not as long as he lived the life of lies he was living. He shrugged off the thought the way he always did. After ten years of practice, it should have gotten easier. Lately, though, it seemed harder than ever.

She'd picked up the bowl of pasta. "Do you want some of this?"

"I can't believe you made it."

"It's passable. Barely. But I had to use canned milk and no butter because—"

"The refrigerator is empty."

"Yes." She lifted her shoulder in a little shrug and carried the bowl to the kitchen. "I didn't know what else to do with my time while you were gone. If I'd had my briefcase…" She set the bowl on the counter and picked up the towel. Folded it. Set it down only to repeat the entire process. "I found the clippers in the garage and was going to try to cut back the roses a little. They need it badly, you know. But the lightning began and it seemed very close, so I—"

"Your Royal Highness."

She went silent.

"Meredith. What's this about?"

She threw down the towel. "What do you mean?"

"If you want to experiment with puttering around a kitchen, fine. Great. Have fun. I'm all for you tackling anything your heart desires. But something's obviously bothering you."

"Besides you?" Her chin had lifted a little, though she still didn't look at him.

He waited. Watched. Saw the gradual erosion of bravado as her shoulders curved.

"Why do you even care?" she asked finally. "You want a wall between us, but you're always scaling it."

"There is no wall, Your Royal Highness."

She cast him a long look, her lips curving humorlessly. "Right."

He grabbed the towel rather than reach for her, and began rubbing at the grease he hadn't been able to get off earlier. "There are things that you don't know—"

She turned to face him. "Then tell me."

"That you can't know."

"Like the fact that you saved Major Fox's life?"

He'd stepped right in that one. He stared at her stonily.

"Oh, never mind," she said tiredly. "The one thing I am good at is research. If I want to find out, I will."

She was good at a great many things, but she wouldn't find anything about that night. Because the RET had made damn sure there were no loose ends. Aside from Fox, that was. The man had been doing his job that long-ago night. Admirably so. And until his health began deteriorating, they'd been able to trust him with the truth. Now, with the disease that sucked at his memories, any truth he'd once known was unlikely to be unveiled or believed.

Which made Pierce feel even more a fraud as he stood in his childhood home. If his father had lived to see what became of his son—

"You can do anything you set your mind to," he told Meredith flatly. He dropped the towel and picked up the bowl, dumped the congealing stuff in the trash, yanked out the bag and tied the ends. He'd take it to the bin rather than leave it inside the house. He had no idea how long it would be before he made it back.

Probably not until after the alliances were signed and done with and life for the RET and the King got back, more or less, to normal.

If the King ever got back to anything at all.

"I can do anything except be a normal woman."

He focused on Meredith, aware that he'd hardly been thinking at all about the King and the state of his health. When that was exactly what should have been foremost in his mind. That, and the uneasy knowledge that Broderick's whereabouts were still unknown. "What are you talking about?"

"I thought I had a fairly decent grasp on what it was like to be a commoner." She picked up the pan she'd already washed and tucked it in the cupboard. "But I was wrong. Do you know I've never been by myself before this afternoon?"

"I wasn't far. And you were perfectly safe. Nobody would connect you with my parents' old home."

"Of course you would have considered the security angle." Her voice was soft. "That's not what I meant, anyway."

She looked naked without her usual aura of self-confidence. Impossibly vulnerable. And it made him hurt because he wanted nothing more than to take her in his arms. "Meredith, you are a compassionate, independent, sensitive woman, regardless of being born to privilege."

"Who does nothing of importance. I don't teach, like your mother did. I certainly don't preach, like your father."

"You don't need to. Your gifts are your own. This country loves you. You're a role model for thousands of girls and young women who see you—an honest-to-God princess—actually doing something productive with your life. None of the Penwycks are purely decorative. Surely you know that."

"But—"

"There are no buts. You are educated, and no amount of privilege can endow you with that. You've gotten the RII involved in efforts beyond their usual scope, and that's no small task. You always represent your family—this country—honorably. You don't have to be able to live the life of a commoner to be able to understand their needs."

She looked away, dashing a fingertip over her cheek. "How independent is it that I didn't like being alone? Knowing that there was nobody within calling distance to come if I needed them. Even at the palace, I've my personal maid. Susan is never more than a moment away. It's pathetic."

"It's natural. It's something you've had no experience with. But you'd get used to it. You'd learn if you had to. If you wanted to. You could do anything you set your mind to, Meredith. But not everyone has it in them to live the life you do.''

"Having my every need tended to? Every indulgence indulged?''

"Living in a fishbowl, nearly every move you make in the public eye. Most people couldn't do it. But you do. And you do it so well that an entire country who feels as if they participated in your growing up loves you for it.''

"I don't want the entire country's love,'' she said huskily. "Just one man's.''

"Meredith—''

"Forget I said that,'' she said hurriedly. "You're not going to admit to anything but what you've already said, and I'm not going to change what I believe, either. So let's just leave it at that before we make more of a mess than we already have.''

"Retreat?''

"After a standoff, what else is there to do?''

"What else is there to do?" Meredith tossed down the newspaper and eyed her father. "I can't help it that someone got a photograph of Pierce and me in his car returning from North Shore yesterday. It's just a photo, Your Majesty. And if it weren't for you canceling your appearance at Sunquest's dedication, I would not have even been there.''

"You look like a drowned rat. You've thoroughly embarrassed this family.''

She wasn't used to her father's censure—had never done anything remotely tending to earn it—and her back went stiff as a post. "We were caught in the rain when his car broke down for the second time near the army base, and I think I'm a little too old for lectures about what is or is not seemly." She'd gone to breakfast particularly early in hopes of catching her father, who occasionally took his breakfast there before his busy day began, but she hadn't expected to receive an earful the moment she appeared.

"It's not as if the photographer caught us in each other's arms," she said reasonably. "Pierce is pushing the car, for goodness sake." And she'd been steering it well off the side of the road where it wouldn't pose a hazard to any driver in the rain. They'd missed dinner with his officers, and she'd never managed to get hold of George Valdosta to cancel their dinner engagement.

Her father sighed noisily and snapped the newspaper flat, clearly a dismissal.

She didn't like being dismissed. Not even by him. "Father, there is something I'd like to ask you—"

"I'm busy, Meredith."

Her jaw tightened. "It's about Uncle Edwin," she persisted.

"He's dead."

"Yes." She would not get sarcastic with her father. It would be beyond disrespectful. "I wanted to know more about *how* he died."

"By a bullet," he said, without looking up. "Why do you care?"

She blinked. She knew her father had never been overly fond of Edwin, but his attitude was far beyond cold. "H-he was my uncle."

"He was a lazy, good for nothing idi— Ah." Morgan was suddenly all smiles and good humor. "Good morning, my dear. This is a pleasant surprise."

Meredith swallowed and turned to see her mother entering the room, followed closely by Mrs. Ferth, who was busy making notations on her steno pad.

"Majesty." Marissa nodded and continued past the breakfast table to the sideboard where she poured herself a glass of orange juice. "I'm not staying, though." She stopped and brushed a kiss over Meredith's cheek. "Come by my office before you leave for the day, would you?"

"Of course." Meredith smiled and murmured a good morning to Mrs. Ferth, and in moments the two women were off again. She looked at the King. "You were saying?"

"Nothing of importance," he said smoothly. He rose, rounded the table and leaned down to kiss Meredith's cheek.

She held herself still, wondering if she was simply going mad as a shiver danced down her spine. "Father, I really want to know more about Edwin's death. There's hardly anything in the papers, and nobody that I've spoken with so far seems to have anything to say about it other than the standard 'unspeakable tragedy' that the papers quote you as having said."

The King watched her, his hazel eyes unreadable. "Let it go, Meredith."

"But—"

"I said, let it go." His voice was silky. "You wouldn't want to cause your mother any pain, now would you?"

"It was ten years ago. Surely long enough for the loss to have been eased by time." Her hands lifted.

"I simply want to know what happened to him. Why are you treating it like some big mystery?"

His face went red, and he grabbed her wrist, yanking her to him. His grip was so tight, her bracelet felt as if it were cutting through her skin. "Are you arguing with me, Meredith? That's not wise of you. Not wise at all. I'm a busy man, with no time for idiotic little quests like yours. The alliances will make history. I'll be known as the greatest ruler Penwyck has ever known."

She blinked, so utterly shocked that she couldn't even twist her wrist free of his punishing grip. Morgan had never been extremely involved in his children's lives, but there had been many times when Meredith and he had engaged in rather spirited debates. He'd always laughed in the end, seeming to delight in her intellect challenging his. And he'd never felt a need to tout his brilliance to anyone.

She lowered her chin, doing everything but dropping into a curtsey. "I'm sorry, Your Majesty." Her voice was husky. Strangled. "I know the alliances are coming to critical junctures. I shouldn't have disturbed you with anything so unimportant."

He glared at her. Then smiled suddenly, releasing her wrist. "That's better." He seemed to consciously relax, and the hard look left his eyes. "I can always count on you to understand."

Meredith watched him walk away, rubbing her wrist gingerly. She'd started out with some vague curiosity about her uncle's death. But the longer it went, the more people refused to speak about it, the more she began wondering. She was no longer merely curious. She was determined.

"I don't understand anything," she murmured softly to the empty breakfast room. "Not you. Nor Pierce. But I will."

Chapter Fourteen

"Hello again, Mrs. Ferth." Meredith kept her tone deliberately breezy as she greeted her mother's secretary. "Is it all right if I go on in?"

"Of course."

Meredith tapped her knuckles once on her mother's office door then entered.

Marissa was seated at her desk, and she set down her pen and folded her hands neatly atop her desk when Meredith crossed the spacious office. "I understand you spent the day yesterday with Colonel Prescott."

"Two in one day."

"I beg your pardon?"

"Father already took me to task," Meredith said flatly.

"He...did?"

"Quite." She was a grown woman. She wouldn't run crying to her mother because her father had been in a foul humor.

Marissa seemed to absorb that for a moment. "Well, darling, I wasn't planning to take you to task. Merely to ask you if things were heading in a more...personal direction for the two of you."

"Personal meaning *what?*" She was still stinging from her encounter with her father, but that didn't mean she needed to take it out on her mother. "I'm sorry." She sighed. "I didn't mean to snap. It's just—"

"The colonel has you confused."

"I...yes. No." She sighed, rubbing her wrist, which still stung furiously. "Not confused, exactly."

"Would you like me to arrange for your father to speak to him?"

"No!" Horrified, Meredith closed her hands over the back of one of the chairs facing her mother's desk. "Promise me you won't do anything of the sort. Pierce's belief in duty is legion. If he's asked by His Majesty to do anything, he probably would, even if he hated every moment of it." Then she saw her mother's expression and blew out a breath. "You're teasing me."

"Perhaps a little. You know your father and I have an agreement not to make arranged marriages for our children."

Meredith laughed shortly, feeling some of her tension abate. She moved around the chair and sat down. "I think the alliances are putting everyone on edge," she murmured. "Even me. I saw Major Fox yesterday up in North Shore. He's living at Sunquest."

"My goodness. I had no idea he was even in Penwyck. He retired ten years ago, at least."

"He doesn't look well. Pierce said he suffers from Alzheimer's disease."

"So, it's *Pierce* now."

"Mother."

"Sorry." Marissa didn't look sorry. Her eyes were positively dancing with merriment.

"So, is that the only reason you asked me to stop by your office? To tease me about the company I'm keeping?"

"Oh, darling. I just wanted to make sure you're all right. I believe I understand how much Colonel Prescott means to you. And I know you are not quite accustomed to men like—"

"You make me sound as if I'm seventeen again."

"You're worldly in many areas, Meredith," Marissa said gently, "but when it comes to your heart…well, darling, you are so very innocent. And to a man like Colonel Prescott, a man who has personally dealt with dangerous situations and individuals, that kind of innocence may hold an immense appeal. I simply don't want you to be hurt."

"Nor does he," Meredith said crisply. "He bends over backward to avoid 'hurting' me. And, really, I'd just as soon not speak of it anymore. If you don't mind."

"Of course," Marissa agreed immediately. "Now, tell me what you have on your immediate plate at the RII. Now that Horizons is open on the army base, I'd like to shift some other duties your way. Unless you're heading into another major project? I know how you prefer that sort of task."

"I'll have Lillian get with Mrs. Ferth, and they can iron out whatever you need."

"Very good." Marissa picked up her pen.

Meredith started to go, but hesitated. She was loath to broach the subject of Edwin with the Queen. But, as she'd told the King, his death *had* occurred ten years in the past. "Mother, there is something I've been curious about lately. I just, well, I just don't know whether I should bring it up, or not."

"Darling, there's nothing you can't talk to me about. Surely you know that."

"Even Edwin?"

Marissa's eyes clouded a little. "What about him?"

"I just wanted to know more about what happened."

"Why?"

Because the mention of Edwin's name makes Pierce's eyes go cold. "You know me. Always curious."

"That's certainly true enough," Marissa said wryly. "What is it that you want to know?"

"He was visiting Majorco."

"On business."

"And…just an accident? The wrong place at the wrong time?"

"Yes."

"That's what Pierce said."

Marissa frowned. "Meredith, is there something else bothering you about this?"

"I don't know." She dashed a hand over her sage green linen slacks. "There are just, well, just remarkably few details about it. About what business he was conducting on Majorco—I mean, forgive me, Mother, but Penwyck wasn't exactly bosom buddies with Majorco back then. It seems as if anything at all involving this family is front-page news, yet the only thing in the papers about *him* were a few very brief obituaries. There were plenty of photos of you and Father, of course. But very little about Edwin.''

''My brother was a private man. We were very close as children, and I loved him dearly.''

Meredith nodded. She was beginning to wonder if he'd been involved in something embarrassing to the royal family. It was the only explanation she could think of that made sense of the oddities. ''I know you did. Father was right when he demanded that I drop it. I shouldn't have brought it up. Major Fox definitely felt for your loss,'' she said. ''He told me so yesterday. Well, he mistook me for you, actually. He said you'd been very kind to him when his wife died.''

''He was devastated when she died of cancer,'' Marissa recalled. ''He retired soon after, I believe.''

A knock on the door brought their attention around. Lady Gwen was peeking in. ''I'm sorry, Your Majesty. Mrs. Ferth has stepped away from her desk. I didn't realize you weren't alone.''

Marissa waved in her lady-in-waiting. ''Come in and sit down, Gwen. Meredith and I were merely visiting.''

Meredith managed a smile, watching the woman smoothly enter and take the chair next to her. Lady Gwendolyn Corbin never did anything that wasn't smooth. She'd raised her daughter, Amira, nearly single-handedly after the death of her husband many years ago, and Meredith had always admired her. "How are you, Gwen?"

"Well, thank you," Gwen assured. Though, privately, Meredith thought her mother's lady-in-waiting looked a bit nerve-racked.

Marissa laughed gently. "The state dinner is less than two weeks away and it is giving her fits, particularly since we absconded with a number of things she'd lined up for the event for use instead during Megan's reception, but she's far too polite to say so."

"To you, Your Majesty," Gwen said, smiling slightly. "There are others, however…"

"Well." Meredith stood. "I'll let you both get to your business. I have to head into the office for a bit before making a run up to North Shore."

Marissa picked up her pen again as Meredith headed for the door. "Darling—"

"Yes?"

"Give the colonel my regards when you see him."

Meredith flushed. "I'm not planning to see him. And I very much doubt that he plans to see me."

Marissa waved her hand dismissively. "Oh, plans. What place do *plans* have when it comes to love?" But her eyes shifted to Gwen when Meredith let herself out of the office. "I need an appointment with His Majesty," she said softly.

Lady Gwen's ordinarily cool expression turned surprised. "Because of Meredith's interest in the duke?"

"No." Marissa stared at the door Meredith had closed behind her. "She's begun questioning the details of Edwin's death."

Gwen looked surprised. "Well. That is unexpected.'' She turned her gold pen over in her fingers. ''It was a terrible loss for you.''

''Yes,'' Marissa murmured. ''And one that was never explained in any reasonable fashion to me.''

''You were devastated. His Majesty undoubtedly wanted to spare you all that he could.''

Marissa mulled that over. It would be just like Morgan to want to protect her. He'd long seemed to think that she needed it. Little did he know the deeds she'd done in order to protect *him* from any pain. ''And what if Meredith's curiosity sets off my own?''

''Has it?''

''I don't know,'' she murmured. ''Morgan never wanted to discuss Edwin, or what happened to him. But every report came back with the same facts. I really can't imagine anything new turning up after all these years.'' She shook her head.

''It was a long time ago, Your Majesty. Some things are better left in the past.''

Marissa's gaze shifted to the other woman. Gwen had lost her husband under rather hushed circumstances, too. They'd both been grieving, and it had cemented a relationship that superseded that of a Queen and her lady-in-waiting. They were friends. ''Do you really believe that?''

Gwen smiled a little, her classically beautiful face looking thoughtful. ''Some days,'' she admitted. Then she opened the pad on her lap and tapped it with the tip of her pen. ''Now. About the state dinner. You had some concern over the seating arrangements?''

Marissa applied one portion of her mind to Gwen's details. Truthfully, she suspected her lady-in-waiting, who was the daughter of an ambassador, could have handled the entire event completely on her own. But there was a certain order to the way things occurred in the palace, and this was one of them.

Nevertheless, when Gwen did head on her way, Marissa called in Mrs. Ferth and gave her instructions to make an appointment for Marissa to see the King. Morgan may have demanded Meredith leave it alone, but he couldn't very well do the same with Marissa.

Her encounter with the King was very fresh in Meredith's mind later that morning as she talked her way past a guard into the underground tunnel that led from the palace to the Royal Intelligence Institute. She couldn't do anything about Pierce's stance when it came to the two of them, but she *could* do something about her questions regarding Edwin. Talking to her mother hadn't helped at all.

"I must verify some information in my father's archives," she told the guard.

"I'm sorry, Your Royal Highness. My orders—"

She smiled confidently. The guard was stone-faced but younger than she, and though she doubted her ability to intimidate him into cooperating, she could, perhaps, charm him into it. "His Majesty won't be pleased if I'm delayed. I'm sure you understand." She was trying to enter the secret, highly secured area from the RII side, thinking she'd have better success. "I've no need to go beyond the archives that are closest to this entrance. I know the tunnel is off-limits to anyone without proper clearance."

"I'm sorry, Your Royal Highness."

Truthfully, she didn't even know what all was

housed in the tunnel beyond the archive she'd had to visit once before. And then for legitimate reasons.

The tunnel was a veritable fortress, impenetrable to unwanted surveillance and to attack. And she needed to get into those archives if she were ever going to be able to put to rest her growing concern over what had happened to her mother's brother.

Despising herself for it, Meredith managed to summon a tear. "Corporal, my father will be so angry with me. Please, couldn't you let me slip in for just a moment?" She brushed her fingertips over the guard's sleeve. "I made a mistake, you see, and—"

The guard sighed and looked over his shoulder down the narrow stairs. The climate-controlled room where the archives were housed was the first door at the base of the stairs. "Just this once." He relented.

Meredith didn't wait for him to change his mind. She darted down the stairs, practically dragging him with her so he could unlock the door. When he did, she smiled brilliantly at him, seeing the way his eyes glazed a little. "You're a love," she said softly, and quickly closed herself in the room. It was filled with shelves, boxes, metal cabinets. Very orderly and very neat.

Which made her work all that much easier, as she quickly made her way toward the appropriate shelves. Painfully aware of the minutes ticking by, she dragged a ladder over and began climbing up the rungs, reading the tidy, discreet labels on the boxes as she passed.

Aronleigh.

Pierce's dukedom. She stared at the box. Began to reach for it. Put her hand on the lid. But after a long moment, she drew back. She wouldn't spy into Pierce's affairs. If he didn't choose to share things about himself with her, then she wouldn't stoop to other means.

She determinedly continued up the ladder, finally finding the box she sought at the very top. "James-ette Bond," she murmured as she pushed off the lid and began flipping through the file folders of every press release the palace had issued in the past twelve years.

She found the official notice from the family in response to Edwin's death. She found the hard copies of the newspaper clippings that must have been on the microfilm cartridge she'd lost. And even though she'd already read through them when she'd visited the library in Sterling, she found herself scanning them again. Looking at the photographs.

Her mother had looked tragic, the devastation at losing her only brother clear on her lovely face. The citizens of Penwyck had bombarded the palace with condolences and flowers. Nobody had liked to see their beloved Queen in pain.

So what if the King had behaved strangely when she'd mentioned Edwin? He was preoccupied. Under a great deal of pressure to insure an economically and militarily healthy future for his country. Bringing up Edwin's passing at this late date was probably fool-ishness on her part.

What she needed was what her mother had said. Another major project. Since Horizons was com-pleted, she was obviously far too much at loose ends.

Sighing a little, Meredith began to slide the file folder into the box, but something stuck in its way.

She reached in, pulling out a folded, yellowed piece of paper. It was a memorandum. She barely had a chance to notice the surprising masthead when she heard the heavy door creak. Meredith did the unthinkable. She shoved the paper into her jacket where it couldn't be seen, then looked down as the guard came into view.

"You were taking so long, I thought you might need some help," he said in such a friendly way that Meredith felt superbly guilty. Particularly with the sharp, folded edge of the paper shoved inside her jacket gouging into her breast.

"Actually, I'm finished," she said, and this time when she tried, the folder slid into its snug place within the box. She replaced the lid and carefully climbed down the ladder. "Thank you again," she said.

The guard nodded and told her he would take care of the ladder. Then he escorted her up the stairs, and Meredith took the elevator to the main floor of the RII and headed straight for her office.

She closed the door, leaning against it, and pulled the paper from her jacket. It crinkled as she opened it, and she let out a shaky breath. She hadn't imagined what she'd seen before the guard interrupted her.

The memo *was* from the RET, and it was directed to His Majesty, the King. It was undated, and contained only a very brief roster of names. She recognized some as members of the Royal Guard. Major Fox, for one. Lady Gwen's deceased husband. But it was the name at the end of the list that jumped out at her.

Army Lieutenant P. Prescott.

She ran her fingertip along the edge of the paper, her thoughts scattered. When her phone buzzed, she nearly jumped out of her skin.

"Colonel Prescott is holding for you on line one. Mr. Valdosta on two." Lillian's disembodied voice sounded through the intercom.

Meredith's fingers crumpled the memo. "Did, um, did the colonel say what it was regarding?" She spoke loud enough that Lillian would be able to hear her.

"No, Your Royal Highness."

Of course he hadn't. She headed toward her desk and picked up the phone. "Thank you, Lillian." She swallowed and stared at the blinking buttons for a moment. She quickly jabbed the second line and canceled her dinner date with George Valdosta. He was understanding, which made her feel wretched, and he was disappointed when she carefully explained that she didn't think she should go out with him at all.

"Is there someone else?"

"There could be, George," she said truthfully. Even if Pierce wouldn't allow himself to be involved with her, the truth was, she simply couldn't bring herself to see anyone else. It had been the underlying reason she'd always remained uninvolved with anyone.

"This isn't about my forwardness the night of your sister's wedding. I apologized for that. I'd drunk too—"

"No, George, it isn't that." She could hardly blame him for being inebriated that night. Not when she'd had too much to drink, also, and emboldened by it had fairly thrown herself at Pierce.

"Well," he said after a moment. "Tell whoever he is that he's a lucky man." Then he hung up, leaving Meredith staring at the blinking button that would connect her to the colonel.

She slowly pushed it.

"Do you have plans tonight?"

Her hands tightened over the receiver. "Good morning to you, too, Pierce."

"Good morning," he said obligingly. "Do you have plans?"

"Perhaps." *Not any longer.*

"Are they breakable?"

"Perhaps." *I already did.*

"Do you have any answers other than perhaps?"

She heard the smile in his voice, and her shoulders relaxed a little. "Perhaps."

"Your parents should have sent you to sit in the corner more often."

Her lips twitched. "What punishments did your parents mete out for your misdeeds?"

"None. My misdeeds came after they died. Will you meet me for dinner or not?"

Her free hand slowly flattened the memo on her desk. It had nothing to do with Edwin's death, but anything that possessed Pierce's name interested her. "Where?"

He named a restaurant in Sterling, and she ran her gaze down her schedule. "That's one of my favorite restaurants," she told Pierce. It had a spectacular view of the Penberne River.

"I know."

She moistened her lips, wanting to see him. Fearing it would be just one more encounter that would end with her feeling bruised. And today, she was feeling rather banged up thanks to her meeting with the King. "All right. I'll meet you there. It'll have to be later, though, as I've got an engagement this afternoon. Maybe eight?" There was no point in him coming all the way to Marlestone to collect her when she'd be traveling from the north, anyway.

"Fine. See you then."

Her fingers tightened around the receiver. "Pierce, what's this about?"

He'd already hung up, though, and all she heard was the dial tone.

She slowly replaced the receiver and tucked the memo she'd taken from her father's personal papers into her purse.

One of these days, she might not jump when Pierce called. But not this day. She had too many questions she wanted him to answer. And she knew deep inside that her questions had little to do with the real reason she kept heading back toward him.

Chapter Fifteen

"I said I liked the open terrace. I didn't expect you to have it cordoned off from everyone but us." When Meredith arrived at the restaurant, it had been to the sight of the owner waiting for her car. He'd directed Bobby to park in the private lot in the rear of the old stone building, before escorting her to the terrace where Pierce was already seated.

He'd risen when she spoke. "I didn't want to be interrupted."

"Obviously. I was brought up the back stairs via the kitchens. It's a wonder the chef and his staff weren't required to wear blindfolds." She sat down when he held her chair and thought she must be imagining the graze of his fingertips over her shoulder before he returned to his seat on the other side of the tiny table.

"You don't look any worse for wear from the rain yesterday."

"Well, my shoes were a write-off." She smiled slightly. "But the rest of me survived. What about your car?"

"I should've sold it long ago. No point in having a convertible if the top won't go up when it rains."

"The car belonged to your parents."

"I don't remember discussing that with you."

"You didn't have to. It's true, isn't it?" She waited for his nod, then picked up the crystal water goblet and looked at the river, which glimmered in the moonlight. "Some things about you are clear as can be. One thing that isn't, however, is what this—" she waved her hand, encompassing the dinner table "— is about. I'm beginning to equate you with hunger. We've had enough meals together, lately."

"Fitting, as I've been hungry for you for years."

She swallowed. Carefully set down the water glass. "What's going on? Why did you ask me to meet you here?"

"Because I know the owner and I can trust that he won't let any avid photographers anywhere near us."

"You saw the picture in the paper this morning."

"My secretary saw it."

"So did the King." She squared the heavy silver flatware with the edge of the table. "He wasn't pleased."

Pierce's eyes seemed to sharpen. "What did he say to you?"

"Nothing I care to get into." She shook it off. "He was in quite a temper, actually, though not necessarily over the photo. He's feeling the strain of the negotiations. We all are.'' She glanced up as a waiter appeared. ''Go ahead and order,'' she told Pierce. ''I'd just like something light. I'm still stuffed from lunch, I'm afraid.''

He did so, and waited for the waiter to retreat before speaking again. ''Speaking of lunch, I hear you went to North Shore this afternoon.''

''Keeping tabs on me?''

''Are you going to throw that dinner roll you've clenched in your hand at me if I admit that I was?''

She smiled faintly and placed the crusty little roll on her bread plate. ''I guess that depends on the reason you were keeping tabs on me.''

''Part of the job, Your Royal Highness.''

She made a face. ''Do you *like* bruising my ego?'' She'd spoken lightly, but Pierce didn't look any more amused than she felt. ''I attended a wedding shower for Lissa Lowell. She's on staff at Sunquest. She's an old friend of mine. I met her fiancé. He's a physician also. Private practice.'' She knew she was chattering but couldn't seem to stop. ''I wasn't going to go, at first, because I had a meeting with the chancelor of Penwyck College. But he canceled. Flu, apparently. It's going around.''

''That's all you went up there for? A wedding shower?''

''Yes. Well, I did stop in to say hello to Major Fox. He's not well at all. In addition to the Alzheimer's, Lissa told me his heart is failing.'' She hesitated. ''He doesn't have long.''

''Did he talk?''

''Yes. He kept mistaking me for my mother, actually.'' She frowned. ''Telling me—her—how sorry he was for Edwin's death. If he'd been more lucid, I would have asked what he remembered about it, since he'd probably been living with his son on Majorco around that time." She shrugged. "As it was, he kept confusing Penwyck with Majorco. It's very sad. I've got Lillian pulling together some numbers on what the RII is putting into research for the disease. Whatever the RII is doing, it isn't enough," she said.

"He's seventy-two," Pierce said.

"And ought to have another twenty years." She toyed with her crystal water goblet. "Lissa—Dr. Lowell—she told me that his son doesn't even visit him. That Major Fox is basically alone. I hate the thought of it."

"He's getting the best of care at the facility."

"I know." She shook her head, sighing. "I told Lissa to call me if his condition changes in the least. I want to be there for him."

"To do what?"

"Just *be* there. He needs someone, Pierce."

"To sit with while he dies."

"If that's the only thing I can do, yes."

His expression didn't change. Meredith couldn't tell if he was displeased. The servers appeared then, setting out everything—salads, steak for Pierce, lobster bisque for her, chocolate ganache—before quietly disappearing again. From below, they could hear the muted sound of other diners and the lilting strain of a piano.

Meredith slipped her spoon into the heavenly bisque. "Now. Why *are* we here?"

"Because I wanted to see you. And you wanted to see me. Otherwise, you'd have never canceled dinner with George Valdosta to see me instead. You're far too polite to put him off twice, even though he deserves it.''

She set down her spoon. ''You knew about my dinner appointment.''

''Dinner date.''

''Whatever.''

''Yes.''

''So, this is what? Some sort of dog-in-the-manger thing? You don't want me, but you don't want anyone else to get near me, either?''

''I think we covered the issue of whether or not I *want* you. The fact that you did meet me here was your own choice, Meredith.''

''I don't think I like you very much right now.'' She pushed away the bisque, what appetite she had gone.

Welcome to the club, Pierce thought. He hated himself. ''I'm sorry,'' he said. And he was. For so many more things than she knew.

Her eyes were guarded, and he couldn't blame her. He needed to be derailing her quest for information about Edwin, but he couldn't bring himself to do it. He'd heard about her trek to the underground tunnel and her little trip through the archives. And while that didn't worry him particularly, what did concern him was her trip to North Shore. But she was so honest. She'd already told him everything he'd needed to know without him having to do the slightest maneuvering.

''I did want to see you,'' he said. ''Just for me. Just because.'' And that really was the unvarnished truth.

''No other reason?''

His eyes met hers, so clear. So true. And everything else just fell away. ''None that matters,'' he said quietly.

Her eyes softened. ''Okay.'' She picked up her spoon and began picking at her meal again. By the time they were wading through the impossibly rich ganache, she was smiling, her laughter soft, rich and full of life, as she told him about the scrapes she and her sisters and brothers had gotten into growing up in the palace.

''You were lucky,'' Pierce said, selfishly absorbing the light that seemed to shine from her. ''To have built-in playmates.''

''Was it lonely? Being an only child?''

He shrugged. ''My parents often took in a church member in need, or a student, for one reason or another. I wasn't exactly alone.''

She watched him, and he knew she saw through the excuse. He had been alone. He still was. And he wondered when it had begun wearing so thin that he could hardly bear it.

She'd set aside her dessert. ''The music is always lovely here.'' Her hair was down, and it stirred in the breeze, seeming to move in tune with the sounds from the piano that drifted through the softly lit terrace. ''Isn't it?''

Music was music. Some he liked, some he considered to be little more than noise pollution. ''Want to dance?''

Her eyebrows rose. ''Here?''

''I need to make up for the spring ball twelve years

ago when I was stupid enough to turn down an invitation to dance with a beautiful girl.''

Her cheeks colored. ''We danced at Megan's wedding reception.''

''That doesn't count. You were tipsy.''

''That's a polite way of putting it,'' she said wryly. ''Every time I looked over and saw you dancing with Juliet Oxford's cleavage, I reached for another champagne. I had a headache the size of the sun the next day.''

He stood. ''Well?''

Meredith eyed the hand he held out to her. ''This isn't an establishment known for dancing.'' But she rose also. And if her hand trembled a little when she put it in his, they both ignored it.

They danced, slowly circling the terrace, under the cloudy night sky with the breeze drifting through, until the pianist downstairs took a break.

And then they returned to the table, and Meredith knew she ought to go, no matter how much she wanted to prolong her time with him. She picked up her purse. Toyed with the clasp, coming to a quick decision. ''Pierce?'' He was standing so close she could inhale the seductive scent of him. It seemed to fill her up. ''Can I show you something?''

He nodded. His eyes were hooded as he drew a lock of her hair from his uniform where the breeze kept blowing it.

She swallowed and opened her purse, pulled out the paper she'd unthinkingly pinched from her father's archives. ''The RET rarely puts anything in writing.''

His eyes narrowed. ''Very rarely.''

"Yet this was." She unfolded it and handed it to him. "Do you know what it's about?"

He looked over the document. "Where did you get this?"

"Does it matter?" She closed her hands over his arm. "I told you I was good at research."

"You're also good at talking royal guards into letting you go where you don't belong."

"You knew."

"Your Royal Highness—" he folded the memo and shoved it in his pocket "—there is nothing that goes on at the palace, the RII or the tunnel that I don't know about."

"And my father."

"Undoubtedly, His Majesty will learn of your little expedition."

She snapped her purse closed and tossed her hair. "I can handle my father." Though her encounter with him that morning left more room for doubt than she'd have liked.

"Can you? Meredith, now is not the time to be poking into old matters. There are more important matters at hand."

It was too much. First her father. Now Pierce. "Are you going to toss around barely veiled threats, too, if I don't cease and desist?"

His eyes sharpened. *"Too?"*

"My father didn't take kindly to my query, either. My mother didn't seem to mind so much, but she didn't shed any new light, either."

"You went to the Queen with your questions." He didn't look at all pleased by that fact.

"Why not? Nobody else will say anything new about Edwin's death."

"There is nothing new to say."

"Well, it hardly matters, anyway." She controlled her rising voice. "That memo doesn't mention my uncle's name. It mentions *yours*. And Major Fox's. What's it about? Does it have anything to do with what Major Fox said about you saving his life?"

He muttered something that sounded suspiciously like "truths." Then he nudged her into her chair and pulled his around to face her, sitting so close their knees brushed. "If I tell you about Major Fox, will you promise to drop this ridiculous hunt of yours?" His voice was barely audible.

She blinked. "I take exception to the label 'ridiculous,' but—"

"Meredith."

"All right." She felt like crying, and it *was* ridiculous. Because the reason she'd been interested in learning more about Edwin was simply that the mere mention of his name made Pierce react. She didn't understand her father's reaction and could only assume it was the stress of the upcoming alliance signings. But when it came to Pierce, she wanted to understand him more than she wanted her next breath.

Her mother had been right about Meredith. She wasn't satisfied unless she picked apart every little thing until she understood it. And she needed to understand Pierce.

Needed to.

"Promise me that you'll keep it to yourself. With the negotiations going on, the last thing we need is for Penwyck to look as if we can't protect our own monarchy.''

She swallowed. ''Pierce, I'd never do anything to jeopardize the alliances. Surely you know that. My father has been living for them for too long.''

His jaw tightened. ''Truer words were never spoken,'' he said wearily, looking around. ''All right. But we can't get into this here.''

''Then where?''

''My flat.''

She rose, feeling shaky. ''Bobby has my car around back.''

He nodded. On the way out, he spoke briefly with the owner and then Bobby, and in minutes they were closed in the utter privacy of Pierce's luxurious flat. But once she was seated on the couch, he didn't seem anxious to pick up the subject.

''Pierce? The memo,'' she prompted after watching him stand at the French doors, looking out.

His expression was inscrutable when he finally turned. ''There was an attempted attack. When I was still a lieutenant, assigned to the palace.''

Her mouth dried. ''An attack on the *palace?*''

''Yes.''

It was inconceivable. Of all the things she'd suspected, *that* hadn't been one of them. ''Why didn't anyone know about it? Why weren't we told?''

''His Majesty knew. The attempted attack was foiled. Obviously. Nobody else needed to know.''

''You did save Major Fox's life, then. During the attempt.'' He looked so impossibly grim as he nodded once that Meredith's eyes flooded. ''Was...anyone else hurt?''

''Yes,'' he said gruffly, ''and no, I am not going to break the King's wishes and tell you who.''

''There were several names on the memo. Were they the people on duty that night?''

''Forget the memo. It's unimportant.''

''We should have been told,'' Meredith whispered. Her mind worked furiously. ''Have there been *other* attempts to harm my father?''

He sat on the stone-topped coffee table facing her, much the way he had faced her at the restaurant. And worry coursed through her when he reached forward to slide his fingers through her hair, drawing it away from her face.

She barely kept herself from pressing her cheek against his hand. ''Have there? This is my *family* we're talking about. I have a right to know.''

''He is the King,'' Pierce said quietly. ''He'll always be a target for some. And regardless of your position, sweetheart, there *are* things you're better off not knowing.''

Her gaze locked with his. ''You're scaring me.''

''No one will ever hurt you, Meredith,'' he promised softly. There was no passion in the statement, only the deadly assurance of fact.

''My father? The rest of my family?''

''Your father is safe. You're all safe. You will continue to *be* safe, because *we're* all doing our jobs.''

''How close did the attacker get?''

He looked pained. ''Meredith—''

''Dammit, Pierce, how *close?*''

Chapter Sixteen

Meredith waited, tense. "How close, Pierce?"

He looked like a man with no patience left. "We caught him scaling one of the walls."

"Of the residence?" Her voice rose, and chills shuddered down her spine.

"It was a long time ago," he said flatly. "Security measures have been completely changed since then."

"That's not an answer."

"It's what I'm telling you."

"It's not enough. Either you can tell me, or I'll make an appointment with His Majesty and find out from him."

His lips flattened. "Don't pull the high-and-mighty-princess routine now. Not with me. Not after everything that's gone on between us."

She was trembling. "He, she, whoever it was got

close. Residence close. And you were involved in stopping it.''

"Meredith, the details don't matter.''

"Of course they matter! It explains everything, don't you see? You were highly involved. And *that's* why the son of a preacher is now the Duke of Aronleigh. Because you're the one who stopped the attacker.''

A hard line had appeared in his lean cheek.

"I'm right.'' She wrapped her hands around his. Rubbed her thumbs over his fists. "Aren't I? You didn't save only Major Fox's life that night. You saved my father's life, too. You saved the King of Penwyck.''

"Yes.'' His voice was clipped.

She sat back, absorbing that. Her gaze slipped over the lovely interior of his flat. She could hear the soft, steady tick of the clock on his fireplace mantel. And she could feel him. His strength. And his pain.

The very fact that she had to drag details from him told her more than anything that his means for stopping the attacker must have been severe.

He was a warrior who prized peace.

"Pierce?''

"Yes.''

"Could I kiss you now?''

His lips twisted. "That's your response?''

"You saved my father's life.'' She smiled shakily. "I think it's merited.''

He let out a long breath. "The kisses I want from you have nothing to do with merit.''

She quickly sat forward, pressing her fingertips over his lips. "Pierce.''

He cocked an eyebrow.

She slid forward another few inches, her knees slipping between his, knocking right up against the hard edge of the coffee table. "Be quiet." When she replaced her fingers with her lips, she felt his smile. It was faint. But it was there.

And her heart simply overflowed.

There was no more hiding from the truth that had been growing inside her.

She loved him.

It took everything Pierce possessed to push Meredith away when he wanted to do nothing more than continue kissing her.

For the rest of his life.

But there were still secrets untold. Secrets that duty demanded he honor.

Even knowing all that, he couldn't fully push her away. He caught her hands in his. Pressed his lips to her palm, battering back the need. Beneath his fingertips, her pulse fluttered wildly through the tender, pale skin of her inner wrists.

Delicate wrists that drew his lips like magnets. That drew a soft, needy gasp from her when he tasted that pulse.

"What happened here?" He gently nudged away the slender, subtly elegant bracelet, baring the thin red scrape that had been nearly hidden.

Her fingers curled as if she wanted to hide it. "Nothing."

"Nothing should mar your skin."

Her eyes were clouded with desire. A rosy flush rode her delicately sculpted cheekbones. And he was two inches away from losing his sanity. "Did you catch your bracelet on something?'' He ran his thumb up her wrist, his need clawing at him as he saw the way her lips parted softly, her eyes darkening.

"The King's grip," she said, her voice barely audible. "Pierce, I can't bear this. Not if you're going to push me away again."

"The King." A tangle of emotion grabbed him by the throat. "What happened?"

"It doesn't matter. I got him at a bad time. He's not quite himself these days." She disentangled her wrists from his hands and slid sideways off the couch. "I have to go."

"You're upset." She looked near tears. "Stay."

"So you can offer your handkerchief before you reject me?"

"I've never rejected you." He'd been protecting her.

"You've been doing so ever since the spring ball when I was seventeen." Her voice was thin, delicate as glass. Just as easily broken. "I should be used to it. But it hurts now more than ever before."

And turning away from his feelings for this unique woman was more impossible now than ever before.

"Meredith—"

"I love you, Pierce."

His words jammed in his throat.

"Maybe I've loved you since I hit my thumb with a hammer at that summer camp and you dashed me off to the kitchen to stick it under cold water." Her lips curved sadly. "I can't pretend that I don't anymore. I just don't have that much strength right now." She picked up her little purse and started for the door.

"Stay."

Her shoulders bowed a little. "Why?" Her voice was raw.

He felt raw, too. "Because I'm not strong enough, either."

She slowly turned to face him. Her arms were wrapped about her middle. As if she need protection. From him. When the only thing he'd ever tried to do in his life was protect her. Protect her family. "You're the strongest man I know," she said huskily.

"If that were true—" he reached her in three long steps "—I wouldn't be doing this."

Meredith gasped when he swung her into his arms and strode down the wide hallway, turning sideways through an open doorway. Her heart climbed into her throat as he set her on her feet and tugged her purse from her numb fingers to toss it aside. She wasn't frightened of him. Never that.

But of the feelings swelling out of control inside her? "I don't want to disappoint you." The words tumbled out of her lips.

His eyes were pure silver as they roved over her. She started, when he settled his hands over her shoulders, his thumbs gliding along the jewel neckline of her sage jacket. "Never," he soothed. His thumbs drifted up her throat, lifting her chin. His head lowered, and all she could see was him. "Never," he said again, closing his mouth over hers.

Sipping. Sensitizing.

Urging her lips apart, going deeper.

Seducing. Slaking.

His hands left her shoulders. Slid over her back. Gathering. Urging.

Her head fell back, her legs unsteady. The only

thing keeping her upright was him. He took her weight, molding her willing curves against him, making her revel in being female where he was male. Soft where he was not.

Then the backs of her knees were against his wide bed, and his fingers were slowly sliding the top button of her jacket free. And the next. She couldn't speak to save her soul. Only feel his knuckles brushing against her breasts as he slowly finished unfastening her jacket and slid it from her shoulders.

She sank her teeth into her lip when his hands went to her shoulders, slipping deliberately beneath the thin spaghetti straps of her pale green camisole. He noticed, bending his head, smoothing his lips over hers in the faintest of caresses. "Don't be frightened."

Her fingers curled into his sleeves. "I'm not," she whispered. She was dizzy with want, fairly desperate to be next to him. Skin to skin. To be with him. "I think you're making me insane."

His lips curved against hers. "Good." The delicate straps slid down her shoulders. Silk slithered, pooling about her waist, caught by the narrow waistband of her linen slacks. His gaze burned over her. And her skin felt hot, too tight.

"I can see your heart beating," he murmured. "Here." His warm palm slid down her throat to the valley between her breasts. She shuddered. "And here." His hand glided, covering her. Shaping her. "So beautiful. Like a dream."

His thumb slid over the achingly taut nipple, and pleasure raced through her. Rampant. Uncontrolled. "If it's a dream, I don't want to wake."

Trembling wildly, she tugged at his uniform. Pulled

it free of his narrow leather belt when her shaking fingers couldn't manage but a few of the buttons. Thrust her hands beneath, skimming over his ribs, sliding up the hard, very real length of his back. Luxuriating in the feel of his flesh, warm satin over steel. "And I don't want to wait," she said on a low moan when he pressed his mouth to her shoulder.

"Heaven forbid the Princess should have to wait," he murmured, his gaze catching hers before he dipped his head and tasted the tight peak his fingers had been tormenting.

Her knees gave way, but he was there, always there, holding her. Catching her. Guiding her to the expanse of his bed where he leaned over her, so broad, so beautiful. She reached for him, but he caught her hands, gently shackling both with one of his.

As if he'd been doing it all his life, he found the hidden zip at her hip, and his palm slid over her waist. Slid beneath the linen, pressing flat against her abdomen, murmuring softly, gentling, when she jerked.

Her legs shifted, restless. Her fingers flexed, needing. His name was a demanding sigh on her lips, and he laughed, low and husky, setting a new flurry of shivers skipping down her spine.

"Good things come to those who wait." His voice was barely a whisper in her ear.

She arched, slid her knee along his hips, thrilling to the way he sucked in a harsh breath and settled his weight over her ever so briefly. Far too briefly. He levered himself off the bed, releasing her wrists, yanking his shirt off and tossing it aside.

Her teeth sank into her lip again as he bent over

her feet, sliding the strappy high-heeled sandals free. Then, in one smooth motion that left her reeling, he dispatched her slacks, silk panties and the camisole. Then, holding her gaze with his, he undid his belt.

And Meredith forgot how to breathe as he finished undressing with that economy of movement that was so much a part of him.

His lips twitched a little, and he knelt on the mattress, leaning over her. Threaded his fingers through her hair and spread it out. "Close your mouth, Meredith."

A flush burned through her, and her mouth snapped shut.

His eyes crinkled, and he kissed her gently. So gently that she would have fallen in love with him right then if she hadn't already done so over the span of years since she'd known him. She settled her hands on his chest, knowing it was *her* that made his muscles jump and his eyes narrow, his gaze going ever more fierce with want.

She pulled at his shoulders. "Come closer," she begged. And nearly cried out again when he complied, his strong legs tangling with hers. Letting her feel him, but not nearly enough. She ached for him, and there was only one way to assuage that. "Now," she demanded, her voice shaking. "Please, Pierce, I can't bear it."

Still he held off. Tantalizing her. Tormenting her. Until she was ready to scream with it, and then, only then, when her senses were already a conflagration, did he slowly press into her.

Holding her gaze with his, fingers threaded through hers, he made her whole.

Tears streaked down her temple, and she kissed him, blindly following where he went, uncaring of the result, only knowing that she'd been made for this. With him.

Then he turned, pulling her over him, his hands on her hips, thrusting deep, letting her find the motion. Eyes glittering as she gasped, overwrought senses hovering on explosion. He arched up, his long arms like bands around her back, his hands tangling in the long waves of her hair. Her head fell back, and his mouth burned over the long line of her throat.

She curled her arms around his hot shoulders, feeling him right down to her soul. She shuddered wildly, gasping for breath, for sanity, for—

She cried out, her body splintering. Barely aware of his harsh groan, barely aware of anything except the mindless pleasure exploding through them both as he took her, impossibly, even further.

And then she couldn't think at all.

Dawn was breaking, the cool gray light drifting over the bed when Meredith opened her eyes, aware that Pierce had left the bed moments before.

Tugging the first thing her hand encountered—his uniform shirt—around her, she slipped from the bed that they'd fairly destroyed over the night and padded silently to the living room.

She found him in the kitchen, phone at his ear. He'd pulled on a pair of jeans, but he wore nothing else, and for a moment, she could only stand there and absorb the sight of him. From his broadly roped shoulders to his strong back. Unable to resist, she snuck forward, feathering her fingertips over the small of his back where she'd learned he was ticklish.

He jerked, turning around, and cupped his hand over the receiver. "Hey. I thought you were sleeping."

She smiled at him in the thin light, slipping her hand over his hard chest, loving the feel of the soft crinkle of hair sprinkled across it. "Not anymore."

He tugged at the collar of the shirt she wore, then dipped his finger down her throat, into the valley between her breasts. "My uniform never looked so good."

She lifted her eyebrow and turned on her heel. "So, what are you doing on the phone, then?" she asked, as she headed back to his bed.

Pierce half laughed, half groaned as he watched her saunter from the kitchen. She was incredible. And sooner rather than later, he'd have to put a stop to what they'd begun. The reasons he'd kept her at bay all these years still existed.

Sobered, he lifted the phone again. "We've got to tell her." He picked up the brief conversation he'd been having with Monteque as if Meredith hadn't just come by and set that gnawing need alive inside him again. "I don't care what we've already discussed. She has to know. Either we do it, planned, or I do it unplanned. This has gone on too long, already."

"I know. Dammit, I *know*." Monteque's frustration carried through the phone, and Pierce understood it only too well. "Fine. Estabon should be the one to tell her. It'll be easier coming from him. I'll get with him about it. He can do it this morning."

Satisfied, Pierce concluded the call and headed to

his bedroom. His conscience wasn't relieved completely. But it was one less lie that he took with him into his bed where the woman he'd loved for years waited.

He stood in the doorway, the sight of her—hair streaming over his pillow, her eyes dark in the silvery dawn—filling up the empty spaces inside him so easily, so thoroughly, that it was difficult to remember the reasons this was ultimately wrong.

Then she propped herself up on her elbow, murmuring his name. She flipped back the sheet, keeping one corner of it modestly about her. "Come back to bed. There are more good things waiting." Her voice was hushed. Impossibly sexy and irresistibly shy.

Could he resist? All night she'd been in his arms. They'd slept only to awaken and make love again. And again. He strode over to the bed, shucking his jeans as he went, and joined her. She slid over to him as if she'd spent a lifetime sharing the space beside him. And for a long moment, he let himself dream of impossible possibilities.

Meredith sighed contentedly. It wasn't often Pierce seemed thoroughly relaxed. But now he did. His fingers lazily combed through her hair, lifting it from her neck, smoothing it down her back. It was soothing and arousing and irresistible. "I may never move again, you know."

A soundless chuckle worked through him. "A little worn out?" He probably should be sorry. She'd been a virgin, and they'd relentlessly made love all night long. She had to be feeling the effects.

"I never dreamed there were so many good things." Her voice was almost demure and gave no hint that she needed or even wanted the slightest reprieve.

"I never dreamed you'd ever be here like this. It's a wonder you haven't given *me* a heart attack."

She pressed her lips to his shoulder. "You're in perfect shape and you know it."

He rolled over, tumbling her onto her back. "You have the perfect shape," he countered with a wry groan. "I've always thought so."

She swallowed, her bones still liquid, and caught his hands when they covered her breasts. "I have a breakfast meeting with the head of PR for the institute."

"Cancel it."

She laughed. Groaned. Sighed. Wriggled around him until he was the one flat on his back and she was hovering over him, her hair a curtain around them. "I can't. Duty, you know."

"Give me five minutes."

Laughter bubbled from her throat, and joy seemed to fill her. "Only five?"

"Ten. Twenty. Sixty." His hands surrounded her waist, and he pushed against her. "You're going to leave me in this state?"

Her giggle turned to a moan as desire rushed through her. She slid down, taking him in. Catching her breath at the way he filled her. Luxuriating in the way his grin turned wicked and his eyes went hot. "Five," she whispered, breathlessly. "Then I've *got* to get a shower and head back to Marlestone. Goodness knows what happened to Bobby all night, I never—"

''Meredith.'' He dragged her mouth to his. ''Tis no time for chatter.''

She laughed softly.

And then there was no laughter all.

Only love, as the room slowly grew brighter, and the two found heaven.

Chapter Seventeen

Marissa took a final look at herself in the long mirror. It was foolish, of course, to be so nervous about having an appointment with her own husband. She'd been married to Morgan for thirty-five years, after all. Surely long enough not to feel a need to powder her nose and primp her hair.

"Your Majesty."

"Yes, Gwen?" She glanced over her shoulder at her friend. "Does this color make me look washed out?"

Lady Gwen tried to hide a smile but failed. "Royal-blue for Her Majesty, the Queen?"

"It's too obvious."

"Of course it isn't. The color suits you extremely well, which you surely know by now. I thought there might be something you should know, before your appointment with His Majesty."

Marissa pinched her cheeks, bringing more color to them. Then, annoyed with herself, she turned to face Gwen. "Yes?"

"Meredith never left Colonel Prescott's flat in Sterling last night. A reporter I know called to warn that someone was peddling a photograph of her leaving his place early this morning. They were looking extremely cozy, apparently."

She caught herself from smiling. "I suppose we'll be in for more gossip."

"Quite possibly."

"Well. At least Meredith must have made some inroads with our stubborn colonel."

Lady Gwen smiled at that, and since Marissa was very nearly running late for her afternoon appointment with Morgan, she excused herself.

Marissa headed out of the residence toward the King's office, located in the public portion of the palace, and nearly bit her tongue with frustration when Sir Selwyn appeared in the corridor, blocking her way.

He looked so serious that her stomach clenched a little. "Selwyn?"

"Your Majesty. I need a word with you."

"The King isn't able to meet with me, after all," she assumed aloud.

"Not exactly." He pushed open a door to an empty office. "Please."

Frowning, Marissa entered. She sat down in one of the leather chairs he indicated. "What's this about?"

"The King," he said. He closed the door, looking distinctly uncomfortable. "Your Majesty, I'm afraid I have some news that will undoubtedly shock you."

Ten minutes later, Marissa was prowling the small confines of the office. "Shock me?" She wanted to screech at Selwyn, but a lifetime of good manners prohibited it. "The man who has been portraying the King all these weeks is, in fact, *not* the King? What on *earth* possessed you to keep such a thing from me?"

"It wasn't intentional," Selwyn said quietly. "Not at first. We fully expected His Majesty to rebound quickly. But one day led to another, and by then we'd brought in Broderick to keep Majorco pacified when they went skittish."

"I want to see him."

"Of course. He's in the infirmary."

"What are you doing to find treatment?"

"The Centers for Disease Control in America is working on it. We have the finest researchers and physicians in the world looking for an answer."

"And none of them know who the patient is."

"No, Your Majesty."

Marissa felt like weeping. She lifted her chin. "Quite a charade you've all managed to pull off. Even I was fooled."

"I am sorry."

Oddly enough, Marissa believed Selwyn, but she was furious. With them. With Broderick, for daring to so much as look at her as if he'd had a right to do so.

However, there was more than fury and humiliation. Both would pass, she knew. She was also terrified. And that wouldn't pass. Not until she knew Morgan would recover.

When Selwyn escorted her down to the excruciatingly well-secured infirmary and into the private room where her husband was being kept, she looked at him through the glass wall separating the unconscious King from a bank of monitors and one uniformed nurse. "I'd like to be alone with him," she said clearly.

Selwyn nodded and spoke quietly to the nurse, who left the room with him.

Left Marissa alone with the King of Penwyck.

Her husband.

A man she loved but didn't really know.

Chewing her lip, she walked around the glass enclosure, pulled up a little rolling stool and sat on it beside Morgan's bed.

He looked so pale. So still.

"Oh, Morgan," she whispered, picking up his hand. Pressing her cheek to it. "What has happened to you? To us? That there be such distance between us that I didn't *know?* I didn't even suspect."

And then the tears did come.

And after the tears, sitting there alone in that room while monitors bleeped and machines sighed, Marissa, the wife, prayed.

"He's dead."

Pierce's head jerked up, his attention ripping from the latest intel reports he'd brought home with him to study. He rose from the couch, turning to see that Meredith stood in his doorway, her face unusually pale. Concern pushed back hard at the tidal wave of pleasure at seeing her. "Your father—"

She wasn't listening. "Major Fox," she said huskily and stepped over the threshold, shutting the door with the same extreme care she must have used to open it without him hearing.

The relief that hit him ought to have shamed him. Of course she didn't know about the King. His Majesty was still in his private infirmary, stable if not conscious, with the Queen watching over him in addition to the highly secure medical staff.

But he was sorry about the major. He rounded the couch, walking over to her. "I know you thought you wanted to be with him."

"I was."

His nerves rocketed to full alert. Not because of her words, but because of the way she moved aside when he reached for her. His arms lowered. Her hair was pinned in a tight coil, and the lines of her uncompromisingly black dress were severe.

The dress left the taut curve of her shoulders and the hollow at the base of her long neck bare, and instead of looking businesslike, she only looked heartbreakingly beautiful. "You were."

"There was a message waiting for me from Lissa Lowell when I returned to the palace this morning." She crossed her arms in front of her, pressing a pad of paper to her chest. "She'd been trying to reach me all night, apparently." Color appeared in her cheeks and her eyes were like feverish emeralds. "I changed and immediately headed for North Shore. He died, peacefully, seven hours after I arrived. He never regained consciousness after a heart attack during the night." She looked brittle. As if one sharp move would shatter her.

"I'm sorry," he said.

Her eyebrows drew together. "Are you?" Her gaze glanced over him, never seeming to settle anywhere.

"Yes. Fox was a good man." He tried to guide her from the foyer, thinking she needed to sit, but again she avoided him. "He served the guards well."

"Protecting the family," she said. "My father."

"Yes," he said carefully, his nerves tightening even more.

"Protecting your secrets."

His eyes narrowed. "Meredith—"

Her head snapped back, and he saw the tears in her eyes. "Your Royal Highness," she said flatly, and slapped the pad she'd been holding against him. "You...bastard. I didn't understand, you know. Why you kept showing up. Kept coming around. After all these years of avoiding me, then, suddenly, there you were. Again and again and again. I was so stupid. It never dawned on me that you were just keeping me—" her voice went hoarse "—preoccupied."

"Meredith—"

"No." She shook her head fiercely. "Don't. Just...don't. You didn't want me to find out your secret, and this was your means of doing it. By using the f-feelings I had for you."

"Which secret?"

Her lips twisted. "Of course. There are so many you must surely be forgiven for not knowing which one!" She waved her hand. "Look at the pad, Colonel. It's right there. Poor Major Fox, rambling as his death drew near. Determined that the nurse who was with him take it all down so he could die with a clear conscience."

Feeling cold inside, Pierce looked at the pad. The

writing was slanted, hastily written. "What was the nurse's name?"

Meredith gaped. "That's all you have to say?"

He'd known there was no future for him and Meredith. No matter what weak insanity had led him to take her into his bed, he'd known better. And the part of him that made him good at what he did kept right on going despite it all. If Fox's last words were as incoherent as the notes on the pad, maybe the situation was still salvageable. Yes, there were some statements that were revealing. But only when viewed with the overall situation. "What do you *want* me to say, Me—Your Royal Highness?"

Meredith's heart was breaking. She wanted him to tell her that he hadn't sought her out for any reasons other than that he loved her, too.

But he'd never said those words to her. Not even when he was so closely a part of her that they'd been nearly indistinguishable. She'd been the one to voice those words. Not he.

"I want you to tell me the truth," she whispered. "If you even know what that is."

"You already know the truth," he said flatly.

"Edwin didn't die in Majorco. He died in Penwyck. And for some...some reason that was important enough for you to pretend an interest in me, you didn't want me finding out that fact."

His face could have been carved from stone. "It was the King's wish."

"That I not find out? It was his *wish* that you distract me, even if the only way you could do it was with your body?" She struggled to control her voice.

"That the location of Edwin's death be kept confidential."

"How nicely phrased. I still don't believe you. My father is an honorable man. He'd never perpetuate a lie. For what reason? To avoid some embarrassment that there'd been a criminal element in Penwyck? It was okay to say that Edwin was in the wrong place at the wrong time as long as the unsavory event happened on Majorco?"

She was so angry she could hardly think straight. And still she was aware that the only thing she wanted was for Pierce to convince her he hadn't used her own feelings against her. That he take her in his arms and tell her she was wrong. That he did love her. That he had all along.

"His Majesty *is* honor. He wanted to protect the Queen. All of it was about protecting the Queen."

Meredith's throat was knotted. "It was ten years ago," she said. "Why does it even matter anymore? Why go to such lengths?"

"I told you I'd hurt you."

"Then how foolish of me to have not believed your promise." She shook her head, turning away. Dashing her fingers over her wet cheeks. "Well, congratulations, Colonel Prescott. You've succeeded in once again making me feel the fool. My own fault, really. I just couldn't get it through my head that what I...felt...was one-sided." She reached for the door, her trembling fingers circling the knob.

"It wasn't."

She yanked open the door, only to jump when he reached over her head and planted the flat of his hand against it, making it slam shut. "It wasn't, dammit to hell, Meredith, it wasn't one-sided. I love you. I've always loved you.''

She leaned against the door because her legs were in danger of giving out. She wanted so badly to believe him. "Then why?"

"Because you were too young. I was a commoner." He shoved his hands through his hair, striding from the foyer into the living room. "Then later, after you came back from studying abroad, I couldn't even be around you without wanting you."

"I wasn't too young then." Her voice was thick. "And you were a duke."

"I told His Majesty I didn't want the dukedom."

"Why?" Despite everything, *because* of everything, she still needed to understand him. "You saved his life from the palace attacker."

Pierce stared at her. He'd moved toward the French doors, as far from her as possible, to keep from reaching out for her even now. But there wasn't enough space in the world to keep him from wanting to reach for her. "You still don't get it, do you? Despite everything, you don't *see*. Your intelligence may be staggering, but your heart is just too good to let you understand the facts even when they're staring you in the face."

She crossed to the couch, closing her hands over the rich leather. Tears stood out on her lashes, diamond bright, each one a stabbing pain in his soul. "Then explain it to me."

"I killed him. All right? I didn't *catch* him. I killed him."

Her brow wrinkled. "The palace attacker?"

"Edwin." He bit the word out. "The palace attacker *was* Edwin. Your uncle. And I killed him."

Meredith swayed.

He rounded the couch and pushed her into a chair before she could sink to the floor. But as soon as he knew she was safe, he pulled his hands back. He didn't deserve to touch her. He'd never deserved it.

From the night when she—little more than a girl dressed in a fancy gown—put her slender arms around him on a ballroom floor. He'd been simply an army lieutenant who knew he had no business touching a princess, much less thinking the heated thoughts about her that had filled his mind. So he'd been unthinkingly harsh with her. And now she was an adult. A beautiful, compassionate, loving woman. While he had the blood of her uncle's life on his hands.

She was staring straight ahead. And already he could see her begin to connect the signs that had always been too obvious for his comfort. "My mother's brother. Scaled the walls of the residence. To harm the King."

"And the Queen."

Her eyes widened, and she paled even more. "What?"

"You need to know the rest, Your Royal Highness."

A tear slipped past her lashes. "Meredith."

He ignored her pained whisper. There was no future for them. He had to start acting on what he knew to be true. Even if it felt like he was ripping out his heart in the process. While it was difficult enough to divulge this particular truth that would finally finish any feelings she had for him, there was one other that wasn't his to share. The truth about her father's health.

He paced. "For whatever reasons, Edwin wanted to throw Penwyck into chaos by removing the King and Queen. Permanently."

"His own sister?" She looked ill. "What about the rest of us? Would he have...never mind. I don't want to know."

"Your mother openly adored Edwin. Penwyck openly adored your mother. His Majesty never wanted her to be hurt by learning the truth. He didn't want the truth to escape and harm her public image. Everything the King ordered was always done in order to protect the Queen."

"It would devastate her," Meredith whispered, nodding. "All over again." She sat up straighter. "This could all have been avoided, you know."

He stopped dead still. "What are you talking about?"

"My looking into Edwin's death. I only grew curious because of the expression you always got whenever someone mentioned his name."

"He'd become a lunatic."

"I think you wanted me to find out."

He stared at her. "That's ridiculous."

"I think it's been weighing on your conscience all these years."

"I'd do it again," he said flatly. "To protect your family. In a heartbeat. And as you've plainly discovered, I'm not the only one who knew the circumstances of that night ten years ago."

"Did you mean it, Pierce? That you love me?"

"Yes." He was incapable of lying about that.

She slowly rose. Moved the few feet to stand in front of him. "I think you believed your secret would always separate us. But the truth—"

"The truth is worse. There is no future for us, Meredith. Whether or not I love you. I killed your *uncle*."

Her fingertips grazed his forearms. "You killed a madman set on destroying my family."

"Dammit, Meredith—"

"Stop blaming yourself," she whispered. Her gaze, like wet emeralds, searched his. "I agree that there is no useful purpose for my mother to ever learn of this. But even if she did, she wouldn't blame you, Pierce. There is nothing my mother values more than her husband and her children. She'd be devastated to know what her own brother had been capable of doing, but she'd never blame you for doing what you had to do to stop him."

"I had nightmares." The words came out before he could stop them. "For years. I'd wake in a cold sweat because I'd failed to stop him in time."

"But you did." Her voice was impossibly gentle.

"Alex Corbin slowed Edwin just enough. But it was close. Too damned close. We never had a chance to interrogate him. Was he working alone? Was someone else in on the plot? It's still a mystery."

She looked a little green. "A mystery ten years gone. If he hadn't been working alone, there would have been some follow-up...efforts...by his partners."

A little green, he thought. But not fearful. She was a Penwyck. And Penwycks were made of stern stuff.

"That was the conclusion the King and the rest of us ultimately came to."

"And your nightmares went away."

His jaw tightened. "Eventually," he lied.

She tsked. "Pierce."

The clock on his fireplace mantel chimed melodically. He focused on it like a drowning man. "It's nearly midnight. How did you get here? Do you have a car down there waiting for you? I'll drive you back."

"I drove myself," she said. "I stopped at the base on my way down from North Shore and was told you'd returned here for the night. Are you going to send me away?"

"Would you go if I tried?"

Her eyes were serious. "If you really don't want me with you, Pierce, then I will go. I won't stop loving you. Not now. Not ever. But I will go because the last thing I want in this world is to cause you pain. You've been causing yourself enough pain all these years by blaming yourself for what you had to do. If being with me makes that worse for you, I will go."

He walked to the door.

Looked over his shoulder to see her standing there. Tears glazing her eyes. Elegant. Strong despite the pain etched in her face.

He reached for the knob.

And he flipped the lock.

Then he turned to her, seeing the way her eyes closed for a long moment in stark relief. And then she looked at him again. And whether or not he believed there was a future for them, in her eyes it seemed he could see forever.

He took her hand and led her down the hall.

Chapter Eighteen

Meredith stretched, her eyes slowly opening to the sensation of sunshine on her face. She pushed up on her elbows, looking around Pierce's bedroom. Flushing a little at the items of clothing scattered about the room. "Pierce?"

There was no response, and she felt a dart of unease work through her. She pushed back the bedclothes and realized he'd left his robe for her at the foot of the bed.

Sliding into it, smelling the faint, seductive scent of him, made her immediately feel closer to him, and she padded out of the bedroom. In the kitchen, she found the note. He'd attached it to the carafe of coffee, and she slowly tugged it free, smiling to herself.

Called to meeting. P.

"Nobody knows more about a life of duty than the

child of a king,'' she murmured. Whistling tunelessly, she poured some coffee into the mug that he'd left out for her and carried it to the bedroom where she began gathering her clothes.

Then she headed for the shower, and clean and dressed, she rode the elevator to the lobby, not caring in the least who saw her leave Pierce's flat. She loved him, and he loved her, and the paparazzi could make of her actions whatever they wanted.

She drove straight to the RII, sailing over to Lillian's temporary desk. "Good morning."

"I think someone had a good night."

"Indeed, someone did." Meredith smiled softly, pouring herself another cup of coffee. "When the colonel calls, put him right through, would you?"

Lillian smiled. "My pleasure."

Meredith tucked her tongue between her teeth, and feeling like she was walking on air, headed to her office. Six hours later, she was heading to the palace. Pierce had yet to call her, but she refused to let that trouble her.

Particularly when she was dashing up the wide staircase toward her chambers and saw the man himself walking out of the King's quarters. She called his name and turned on her heel, skipping down the stairs.

Pierce glanced at the door Broderick had barely kept from slamming shut in his ire. The RET had kept Broderick busy all day, and Broderick hadn't appreciated having his own agendas turned upside down for theirs. But the door was safely shut now. The Queen knew the truth. And Broderick's charade would be over once the alliances were signed. The

RET would slip the man back into the life of secluded privilege from which they'd pulled him.

Pierce looked at Meredith, smiling at the way she suddenly seemed to realize she was practically running and deliberately moderated her pace. Her eyes were glowing, and though he'd spent the entire day telling himself he needed to break things off with her, he couldn't bring himself to say a single word to that effect. "Hi."

She stopped in front of him, somehow managing to look both sexy and shy at the same time. "I missed you this morning."

"Meetings."

"So your note said. I don't mind," she said easily. She stepped closer, smoothing her palm up and over his chest. "Though I'd have preferred to share the shower with you. But maybe next time."

"I've created a monster."

Her green eyes were laughing. "Would you change it if you could?"

The only thing he'd change would be the necessity of keeping the truth about her father from her. As long as he had to maintain that lie, pursuing a relationship with Meredith was impossible. "You're perfect just the way you are."

She moistened her lips, and want streaked through him. "Stay and have dinner with us. Would you please?"

"With the family? Meredith, that's not a good—"

"Please. They're not *that* bad."

Pierce swallowed hard when she pressed herself against him and bold as brass nibbled at his chin. "Please?"

"Using your feminine wiles?"

"Trying. Is it working?"

His hands slid to her hips, pulling her against him. Tight. "What do you think?"

Her eyes went slumberous. "Working beautifully," she whispered on a sigh. "Stay with me."

"I want to."

"Do I hear a but in there?"

"Meredith, your mother—"

She pressed her lips to his, silencing him. Then she leaned up, murmuring near his ear. "She will never, ever have to know about Edwin. I told you that last night. You were right, Pierce. About everything. Knowing what he did, what he tried to do, oh, it wouldn't serve any good purpose. And sooner or later, the public would find out, and she doesn't deserve that, either."

He threaded his fingers through her luxurious hair. "You are a remarkable woman."

"Who loves a remarkable man," she whispered. "Now, please. Stay for dinner?"

He couldn't resist her. He'd tried for too many years, and he'd failed. And right then, with her body soft and warm against him, he couldn't deny her again. "All right. I've got to clean up first."

"That's okay," she whispered. "My shower is large—"

"Meredith." He kissed her hard and quick and deliberately set her away from him before she could make him forget any semblance of common sense.

She laughed softly and headed for the stairs once more. "You've got three hours. Plenty of time to go back to your flat. And Pierce—"

"Yes?"

She smiled impishly. "Don't forget your tooth-brush." She laughed at his strangled groan and darted up the stairs.

When he returned later that evening, she was still laughing. He stood in the entry to the family room where one of the butlers had showed him and watched Meredith across the room. She was standing next to Owen, her head tilted back, musical laughter bubbling from her lips. He watched her slowly look his way, as if she'd sensed him there. And her expression was so warm, so full of love, that for a minute, he couldn't see anything but her.

Couldn't feel anything but the wave of welcome that emanated from her.

Then she crossed the floor, tucking her hand through his arm and pulling him into the room. "Everyone will be here except the King. He doesn't often have meals with us these days."

Pierce kept his smile in place with an effort. How had hiding his lies ever become so difficult?

"And you know everyone, of course. So there's no point in introductions."

Owen stuck out his hand. "Colonel. Glad you could make it."

Pierce shook the prince's hand. He'd always liked Owen, but unlike so many of his countrymen, he didn't make the automatic assumption that the young man would, in fact, one day be King. There were two sons, after all. "Thank you, Your Royal Highness."

"Oh, please." Anastasia laughed and, as natural as you please, brushed a welcoming kiss over Pierce's cheek. "We don't stand on that much ceremony. Not in here."

Owen smiled crookedly. "She's right. Would you like a drink? Sherry?"

"He likes beer," Meredith said for him.

"Thank God," Owen muttered. "Another male who doesn't drink that god-awful sherry."

He'd just accepted the cold bottle from Owen when the Queen appeared in the doorway, looking as regal as ever, despite the fact that she'd spent most of her day tucked in the bowels below ground with her comatose husband.

But then, the Queen had always been stronger than most people gave her credit for.

She walked right to him and looked him in the eye. "You love my daughter."

"Mother." Meredith's hand, tucked in his, tightened.

"It's all right, Meredith." He wouldn't turn away from the Queen. He'd been doing that for far too many years. "Yes. I love her."

Marissa smiled faintly. "Then welcome," she said gently. And, as Anastasia had done only moments before, she stretched up and brushed a kiss over Pierce's cheek. "It is time for the secret to be shared, isn't it," she murmured, her gaze meeting his meaningfully.

Pierce's throat knotted. And when the Queen continued to look at him, he knew what she was really saying. The gift she was giving. Whether he had the agreement of the rest of the RET or not, she'd given him the only approval he cared about. "Yes. It is time."

"I don't think it's any secret that you and my sister can't keep your hands off each other," Owen drawled, and everyone chuckled. Marissa turned away, breaking that meaningful look as she accepted a glass of the dreaded sherry from her son. Only Pierce knew the secret to which the Queen had been referring was not his relationship with Meredith, but the truth about the King.

And he knew then that no matter how heinous he'd found it to kill a man with his bare hands, he'd do it again, if only to protect this family from harm.

Not because of duty.

Because of love.

"Are you all right?" Meredith touched his face.

"Yes." He grabbed her and kissed the palm. "I think I am."

"Good. Because dinner is ready."

"Wait."

Her eyes danced. "I think you should eat, Colonel," she suggested in a low voice. "You might have reason later to keep up your strength."

"I have something to tell you first." He drew her over to one of the couches and nudged her down.

Her expression went wary. "What is it?"

"Nothing bad." He'd tell her later about the King. He'd take her down to see her father himself. Give her a chance to adjust. She'd probably give him grief for not telling her sooner and then probably turn right around and make him accept the reasons he hadn't been able to do so.

She lifted her eyebrows. "Well?"

"Marry me."

Her eyes went wide. Soft as dawn. "I...Pierce."

"I mean, please. Will you marry me? I wouldn't want you to think I'm trying to order you around, or anything."

Her eyes glistened. "You're the only one who could order me right up to the altar," she whispered. "I didn't think you wanted that."

"Because I did a damned good job of convincing you otherwise." He started to kneel, but she shook her head, tugging him instead to sit beside her.

"I want you beside me. All the way."

"I'm not an easy man."

"Are you trying to warn me off now that you've both demanded and asked for marriage?"

"I don't want you to regret anything."

"The only thing I regret—" her fingers twined with his "—are the years we spent dancing around each other, when we could have been dancing with each other."

"I'm not good enough for you. I never have been."

"Be careful what you say. You're talking about the man Her Royal Highness, Meredith Elizabeth, Princess of Penwyck, plans to marry."

"Be very sure, Meredith. Because I won't be able to let you go. It was hard enough when I didn't really have you. It'll be impossible once I do."

"You've had me all along, Pierceson Prescott. Whether you wanted me or not. I was always yours. And yes, I'll be your wife. I want a life with you. Children with you. But mostly—" she leaned toward him and pressed her lips to his "—mostly, I just want you."

He slid his arms around her. "I must have done

something in this world right," he murmured, sipping at her lips. "That you'll have me."

"Oh, I will definitely have you," she said, her voice as rich with laughter and love as her eyes were filled with tears. "And you'll have me, as well." She kissed him, and her breath was unsteady when she stood. "Come with me."

He stood, also, pulling her against him. Right where he wanted her. More or less. "Meredith, your family is very welcoming. But I can't go into the dining room in this state."

"Who said we're going to the dining room?" She pulled him into the hallway and headed toward the grand, sweeping staircase that led to the upper level where her chambers were located. "There are better things to feast on than rack of lamb or whatever menu Chef has planned tonight."

He caught her around the waist, drawing her close to him. "Like what?" But he already knew.

Her lips slowly met his, and at last it sank in just how much he'd been lost without her.

"Love," she whispered, holding him. Heart to heart. Soul to soul. "Tonight, darling Pierce, we feast on love."

Epilogue

"My, my, my. Look who has come to breakfast."
Anastasia giggled, and Meredith sighed mightily,
pulling Pierce into the breakfast room.

"I thought you said we wouldn't run into anyone
down here," Pierce murmured for her ears alone as
he followed her over to pour himself some coffee.

"Sometimes even I am known to be wrong." Meredith laughed softly, loving the dusky tinge climbing
along his hard jaw. "I figured they'd all be gone by
now. It's later than usual."

"They'll know I spent the night here with you."

"And they'll get used to it," she whispered. "I'm
not ashamed of it. Are you?"

"Hell, no." His eyes roved over her, and this time
it was her face that felt flushed. Then he smiled a
little, and she felt like laughing right out loud, she

was so happy. So full of joy. Not even a midnight trip down to an infirmary that she'd never known existed had been able to quell the deep, abiding joy she felt at knowing she would be spending her life with Pierce. She'd been startled to see her father incapacitated. And oddly grateful that the oddities she'd thought she'd lately noticed in him were because he hadn't been *himself* at all. And she had absolute faith that her father would recover.

She pulled Pierce to the table and they sat down to eat. "Where is Owen?" she asked her sister.

"Out. As usual." Anastasia slid into her seat and poked at her bacon with a fork. "He probably went out to find some entertainment of his own after dinner—which some people managed to miss, I might add—last night. That boy seriously knows the meaning of sowing his wild oats."

"Anastasia." The Queen entered the room, chiding. "Such a thing to say."

"Well, it's true, isn't it? Goodness only knows what Dylan's out there doing, as well."

Marissa tilted her head, considering that. "Boys will be boys." Her blue gaze drifted over Pierce. "And men will be men. Good morning, Pierce."

He'd stood the moment she'd entered the room. "Your Majesty."

"Marissa will do," she said softly, lightly touching his shoulder as she passed behind him to pour herself some tea.

Meredith squeezed Pierce's hand and tugged him back down to his seat. She knew how much he admired the Queen and how deep his loyalty to her father, the King, went. She understood so much more than ever before just what kind of man he was. He'd been awarded a noble title by her father as a result of the events that long-ago night when Edwin had attempted his inexplicably horrible deeds. But Pierce had been noble to his core well before that. His nobility was born of the heart. It always had been.

"So, are we going to hear wedding bells ringing through all of Penwyck again before long?"

Meredith caught Pierce's gaze at Anastasia's teasing words.

"They'll definitely be ringing," he said, looking utterly content and supremely male.

"We're not in any hurry to start with the details," Meredith said. She loved Pierce, and he loved her. And for now, that was more than enough.

"Too busy just enjoying each other, I suppose," Anastasia remarked. "Well, might I remind you that neither one of you is getting any *younger?*"

Pierce laughed softly when Meredith let out a most unprincesslike snort. "You're also on the downhill slide to thirty, my dear," she told her sister sweetly.

"Yes." Anastasia smiled brilliantly. "But my speed is a lot slower than yours, darling."

"Girls," Marissa tsked. "Behave yourselves, or Pierce will think we're a totally undisciplined family." She noticed Selwyn had silently appeared just inside the doorway and set down her tea before going to him.

"The sooner it is legal, the happier I'll be," Pierce said truthfully. But his gaze was focused on the Queen, who looked suddenly pale. Selwyn entered the room, and the Queen suddenly ran from it.

Meredith and Anastasia popped up from their seats,

expressions concerned, and Pierce rose more slowly, sliding his arm around them both. "Estabon? What is it?"

"It's Owen," Selwyn said rapidly, allaying Pierce's concern that the other man had come to deliver bad news about the King's health.

Selwyn didn't look at the princesses. He looked straight at Pierce, and his gaze was dark. Grim. Speaking of things the RET had prayed would never occur.

"It's Owen," he said again. "He's been kidnapped."

* * * * *

*If you're longing for more
royal love and scandal,
don't miss next month's
Silhouette Special Edition,
ROYAL PROTOCOL,
by Christine Flynn,
the third book in the
CROWN & GLORY series.*

*Silhouette presents an exciting
new continuity series:*

**When a royal family rolls out the red carpet
for love, power and deception, will their
lives change forever?**

The saga begins in April 2002 with:

The Princess Is Pregnant!

by Laurie Paige (SE #1459)

**May: THE PRINCESS AND THE DUKE by Allison Leigh
(SE #1465)**

**June: ROYAL PROTOCOL by Christine Flynn
(SE #1471)**

Be sure to catch all nine Crown and Glory stories: the first three appear in
Silhouette Special Edition, the next three continue in Silhouette Romance
and the saga concludes with three books in Silhouette Desire.

And be sure not to miss more royal stories,
from Silhouette Intimate Moments'

Romancing
the Crown,

running January through December.

Where love comes alive™

*Available at
your favorite
retail outlet.*

Visit Silhouette at www.eHarlequin.com   SSECAG

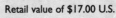

If you enjoyed what you just read,
then we've got an offer you can't resist!

Take 2 bestselling
love stories FREE!
Plus get a FREE surprise gift!

Clip this page and mail it to Silhouette Reader Service™

IN U.S.A.	IN CANADA
3010 Walden Ave.	P.O. Box 609
P.O. Box 1867	Fort Erie, Ontario
Buffalo, N.Y. 14240-1867	L2A 5X3

YES! Please send me 2 free Silhouette Special Edition® novels and my free surprise gift. After receiving them, if I don't wish to receive anymore, I can return the shipping statement marked cancel. If I don't cancel, I will receive 6 brand-new novels every month, before they're available in stores! In the U.S.A., bill me at the bargain price of $3.80 plus 25¢ shipping and handling per book and applicable sales tax, if any*. In Canada, bill me at the bargain price of $4.21 plus 25¢ shipping and handling per book and applicable taxes**. That's the complete price and a savings of at least 10% off the cover prices—what a great deal! I understand that accepting the 2 free books and gift places me under no obligation ever to buy any books. I can always return a shipment and cancel at any time. Even if I never buy another book from Silhouette, the 2 free books and gift are mine to keep forever.

235 SEN DFNN
335 SEN DFNP

Name	(PLEASE PRINT)	
Address	Apt.#	
City	State/Prov.	Zip/Postal Code

* Terms and prices subject to change without notice. Sales tax applicable in N.Y.
** Canadian residents will be charged applicable provincial taxes and GST.
All orders subject to approval. Offer limited to one per household and not valid to
current Silhouette Special Edition® subscribers.
® are registered trademarks of Harlequin Enterprises Limited.

SPED01   ©1998 Harlequin Enterprises Limited